The Mysterious Unraveling of Paulette's World

Angela Wright, Ed.D.

ISBN 978-0-578-89986-2

Printed in the United States of America

Dedication and Acknowlegments

This book is dedicated to trauma survivors and girls like Paulette who have or still are experiencing moments that just seem to never end. There is hope. Answers may not seem to be readily available, but God is always near to get us through the storm. Never give up!

I wrote this book in remembrance of my mom and want to acknowledge both my mom and dad (Robert & Diane Cornelius). Also, thanks to my editor Darcy Crosman, EdD, and my family and friends for supporting me through this process. I also want to give a shout out to Ernie Hudson, who I worked alongside while speaking at Fresno City College.

Table of Contents

Chapter 1: The Morning After

The bitter cold night her parents run off leaving her with enough food to last a week, Paulette cries and wonders why they would leave her. Paulette lives in downtown Chicago where she walks to school every morning. That morning, she begins her usual routine of getting ready for school despite the fact that her parents are gone. It's the last day of school for the week and she tries to believe that it's a normal day and what has happened hasn't really happened.

While walking to school, Paulette is approached by several individuals, people offering her drugs, and pimps asking if she is looking for work. It's almost as if they know she is all alone in the world now. Paulette feels so vulnerable. She begins walking faster and faster until she is almost running toward the school. She runs while shreds of snow whirl around her. She is fighting back tears as she walks into her first class, which is already in session. Paulette usually sits in the front of the class; however, today she finds herself sitting closer towards the back. Mr. Temple, a short, balding man, sees her as she sits down. She notices his face reflects some concern but she doesn't know why. Several classmates turn and look at Paulette, and Paulette feels like sinking into her seat as a wave of heat flushes over her body. After school, Paulette quickly rushes towards home. She begins searching the house for a note from her parents in hopes of finding out when they will return. Paulette finds an envelope addressed to her from her grandfather tucked in a small compartment of her mother's drawer. Paulette's grandfather died when she was 5 years old. There is a bond for $2000.00 with her name on it and a note attached that reads, "My dear Paulette you are somebody special. You can do and be anything you want to. Remember God will always love you." Quickly Paulette sticks the envelope in her pocket and continues to sort through items.

As evening falls, Paulette begins to feel exhausted. She decides to lie down on the couch to shake off her feelings of confusion. Around 6 that evening, she hears a knock on the door. For a moment, Paulette doesn't move. However, she also doesn't want to sit in this house alone and maybe there's some word from her parents. With a look of dismay, Paulette slowly walks towards the door. She pulls aside the curtain, and to her surprise, Mr. Temple is standing there patiently waiting for the door to open. Paulette does not want to answer. She paces the floor for a bit, wondering whether she should open the door. When she finally opens the door, Mr. Temple greets her warmly and asks if he can come in. After entering the house, Mr. Temple begins to look around, and he seems to sense that Paulette is nervous. He tells Paulette that he would like to speak to her parents. Paulette looks at the floor and mumbles, "My parents aren't here." Mr. Temple looks surprised. He asks, "When will they return?" Paulette shrugs her shoulders and continues to look at the floor. On hearing this response, Mr. Temple's face looks troubled. He seems to sense that something here is very wrong.

"Paulette I am not sure what's going on, but you are more than welcome to stay at my house until there is a resolution to the problem," Mr. Temple finally says, "I promise to help you in any way I can, but you have got to be honest with me."

That evening Mr. Temple and Paulette go to Subway, one of Paulette's favorite places to eat. Mr. Temple drives Paulette home around 8 that evening. Before getting out of the car, Paulette thanks Mr. Temple for dinner and assures him her parents will be home later that night. Mr. Temple watches as Paulette walks into the house. Paulette feels better knowing she has somebody who is willing to help her.

Mr. Temple, still in his car, hesitates to leave. He decides to go back to the house and sit with Paulette for a while before heading home. Paulette is on the couch begining to finish the other half of the sandwich she still has from Subway. After a few bites, Paulette falls asleep. Paulette's parents do not return and Mr. Temple senses something really is wrong. He also knows that Paulette will never tell him the truth.

Mr. Temple pursuades Paulette to return with him to his house until her parents return. The next morning, Paulette awakens in a beautiful, cozy bed. The furnishings of the room grow bright in the light of day, giving her a comforting feeling. The aroma flowing through the air reminds Paulette of her grandmother's cooking. When Paulette would visit her grandparents in the summer, her grandmother would cook breakfast for Paulette every morning.

Paulette stays at Mr. Temple's for 2 weeks or so, and she no longer anticipates she will hear from her parents. One Saturday afternoon, Paulette hears Mr. Temple calling her name. It's Tina, one of Paulette's classmates, at the door. Paulette has been growing close to Tina over the past few weeks. Still, Paulette is surprised that Tina is visiting her because Tina never told her she was coming over. But she's happy to see her and doesn't give it much thought. Before she runs down to greet Tina, she sees Tina and Mr. Temple having a hushed conversation in confidence. Paulette knows something weird is going on, but she is unable to put her finger on what. She signals for Tina to come up the stairs. "Well?" asks Paulette.

"Well what?" Tina asks.

"What were you guys talking about?" asks Paulette.

Tina is standing that certain way she does when she feels she has everything under control. "Don't worry," Tina smirks, patting Paulette on the back and plopping down on the bed." Paulette can't believe that there's anything to worry about at this moment. Tina is here, and for the first time in a long time, Paulette feels safe.

On the following Saturday, Paulette realizes what both Mr. Temple and Tina had been up to: A surprise birthday party for Paulette! Turning 16 is a high time for her. But then, soon after the party is over, she notices a strange look on Mr. Temples face. They are sitting at the table. "What's wrong?" Paulette asks. Mr. Temple begins to respond but then simply looks down. Paulette, feeling nervous, says, "There has to be something wrong. Nobody looks so down for nothing." Paulette sits down in Mr. Temple's black rocking chair that his grandmother left behind when he was just 2 years of age. Paulette begins to shuffle both of her feet back and forth. Mr. Temple then says, "Paulette, I have something to say to you. I do not know how to say this, but before you can stay here with me, there are procedures." He continues, "Social Services wants to know whether there is any other family that you could stay with." Paulette is aghast, "What?" she gasps. "You called Social Services?" She feels this is a betrayal.

"Mr. Temple I have not been very honest with you," Paulette begins to explain. "I have a grandmother, and I have been trying to call her since the day my parents left." She pauses and adds, "Her phone line is disconnected. I wanted to go and stay with her, but since I came here and have been getting close to Tina, I just wanted to stay here with you." Paulette begins to cry. She looks at him with desperation in her face: "Please let me stay here with you! We can contact my grandmother some other time. She would be fine if I'm here with you! I know she would. I just haven't been able to reach her."

Mr. Temple shakes his head and says," "Paulette I am sorry. I have to talk to your grandmother. This is protocol." Paulette lets out a heavy sigh. He continues, "Social Services will be here on Monday to pick you up and I'll do my best to get you back as soon as I can talk to your grandmother." Paulette continues to cry silently and Mr. Temple pats her on the shoulder. He tries to comfort her, saying, "You will only have to stay with them a couple of days until things are settled." With those words, Mr. Temple kisses Paulette on the forehead and shuts the door behind him as he goes to his room.

At that moment, Paulette feels betrayed. Her heart feels as though someone has pierced a knife straight through her heart. She is thrown into a dark place within herself. She is bereft and the pain is unbearable. There is no sleep for Paulette that night. She tosses and turns, and just before the break of day Paulette remembers Tina's words. Tina told her that if she ever needed anything to just let her know. Paulette jumps out of bed, runs to the phone and frantically dials Tina's number. Tina answers the phone on the second ring. "Tina I need your help," Paulette whispers. "Who's this?" Tina asks. "It is me," Paulette responds. "Me who? and do you know what time of the morning it is whoever this is? Tina asks. "Enough games. It's me, Paulette."

"You should have said so! And why are you whispering?" Tina asks.

Paulette responds, "I'm going to my grandmother's house, but there is only one problem. I only have the $25."

Tina asks, "Let me guess. You would like to get the rest from me?"

"Tina, you are such a friend," says Paulette. "So we have the money. That part is resolved. There be one problem. How am I going to get it from you?" Paulette asks.

Paulette does not ask Tina where she's going to get the money, but Paulette knows Tina will not let her down. "I have an idea," Tina responds. "I will have my father drop me off at Mr. Temple's this morning for school." She continues, "I will tell him I'm going to school with you."

That morning Paulette hears someone knocking at the door around 6 o'clock. Mr. Temple, in the process of finishing breakfast, invites Tina in. Paulette is unable to eat her breakfast, so

Tina eats her portion. Paulette thinks, *For Tina to be so small, she sure can eat.*

"Tina, what brings you out this way so early in the morning?" Mr. Temple asks.

"I decided that I would ride to school with Paulette today. You know, being that this may be our last time seeing each other," Tina responds. A startled look crosses Mr. Temple's face. Wanting to ease fears that Tina may have of Paulette's imminant removal to social services, Mr. Temple, replies, "that seems unlikely.

On the way upstairs, Tina moves past Paulette in a rush to get to the bathroom. Paulette goes to her room to continue packing. Some minutes later, Tina is still in the toilet. Paulette knocks on the door, saying, "Is everything all right in there?" All Paulette can hear is coughing and gagging. There's no answer. Several minutes pass, and the door finally opens. Paulette asks Tina, "Are you all right"?

"Yeah," Tina responds. "I just felt a little sick." Paulette looks at her with true wonderment and asks, "How can you just barf down breakfast and now be sick?" Tina responds simply,"It happens to the best of us," and then hastily adds, "Enough questions. How much money do you need?" Then she voices an idea that suddenly occurs to her, "Say, Paulette, how about we skip school and go back to my place? We can just hangout and listen to music by the pool before you leave."

"That sounds like a magnificent idea," Paulette responds. "Let me grab a couple more things." She adds, "I called earlier this morning to check bus schedules and my bus leaves at 9 o'clock tomorrow morning. I will purchase my ticket then."

Tina wonders, "Paulette, what are you going to tell Mr. Temple? He's going to be worried."

Paulette replies,"What do you mean Tina? I'm not going to say anything."

"Paulette there is something I have to tell you."

"What is it, Tina?"

"When we gave you that birthday party, it was not my idea."

"I know."

"How do you know?"

"I think Mr. Temple wanted to make me feel better. I knew something was up. A gorgeous girl like you hanging with a poor girl like me?"

Tina smiles and says, "Paulette. I just want you to know I enjoy you being my friend, and that is the truth. Money does not matter to me." Tina adds, "I'm so glad we're friends." Tina gives Paulette a hug while waiting for the chauffeur. Paulette looks down for a minute and then breaks out into a smile and responds, "Me too."

Before Mr. Temple leaves for school, Paulette tells him she is not feeling good and wants to stay home, and Tina calls her mom and does the same. Mr. Temple looks at Paulette and from the look in his eyes, he seems to know Paulette is not telling the truth.

The chauffeur is waiting and they climb in. Tina is an only child. "It must be nice," Paulette thinks aloud. Tina is quiet for a moment. Then she says, "Let's go swimming as soon we get to my house." Paulette can tell when Tina does not want to talk about her feelings. Tina always changes the subject whenever Paulette inquires into anything she might be feeling. Paulette now though is full of excitement. Spending the day with Tina is going to be fun. She can put off thinking about tomorrow and the day that lays before her seems endless. Then she remembers. "Tina I would love to go swimming, but I have no swimming suit."

"No problem. You can wear one of mine. You can take your pick." After reaching Tina's house, Tina runs to her room, opens her top dresser drawer, and asks Paulette to pick out a suit. "I cannot wear any of those swimsuits."

"Why not?"

Paulette frowns as she responds, "Bathing suits always make me look like I am dressed in a pole."

"Paulette we are going swimming, not boy shopping. Wear that one!"

Paulette takes the suit and before she can begin to get into it, Tina is in her suit and takes off running towards the pool. Paulette quickly changes and heads towards the pool and then suddenly remembers she cannot swim.

Tina calls out, "Come on in what are you waiting for?"

Paulette is too embarrassed to say she cannot swim, so she plays as if she is testing the water. "Say, what are you waiting for Christmas?" Tina is always hyper. She looks at Paulette and asks, "Can't you swim?" Paulette looks away shyly and responds, "No." "That's okay, I have a life jacket you can wear," adding when she looks at Paulette's fearful face, "I promise you will not drown." After splashing around in the water, Paulette thinks to herself that this day is better than her sixth birthday. Paulette has never met Tina's mother, who stays in her bedroom the whole time. Talk about strange.

"What are you thinking about?" Tina asks.

"Oh, nothing," Paulette responds.

"Come, Paulette, you can tell me."

"Well, now that you ask, I was wondering why I have not met your mother."

"Say, how about we get some ice cream?"

Why doesn't Tina want to talk about her parents? Time is going by fast. They eat dinner at 6 p.m. without any parent being present, and Tina says, "Paulette, you never did say how much you would need to purchase your ticket." Paulette looks away as she murmurs, "$65."

"What?" Tina asks. "It sounded like you said $55."

"No, I need $65."

"Is that all?" Tina responds, "That is the cheapest loan ever." Paulette is relieved.

When Tina gives Paulette the money and a big hug, she tells Paullette, "Don't worry about paying me back. When the time comes, it will take care of itself." Paulette has no clue what Tina is talking about, but for some weird reason, Paulette feels she will one day know what Tina means.

Later on that night, Paulette and Tina begin washing up for bed, and the funniest thing happens. While brushing their teeth, they both look over at each other. "Tina," says Paulette.

"Yes, Paulette."

"Do you ever feel alone?"

"Yes I do."

"I feel that way all the time," Paulette responds. "Look Paulette, what we have found! We now have each other! Promise me you will keep in touch with me." Before the night is over, Tina and Paulette become blood sisters and then off to sleep they go.

The next morning Paulette awakens to a loud clanging noise. Tina's bedroom windows are getting washed. Paulette feels somewhat funny. The workmen can see right through the curtains.

Paulette begins getting ready to leave for her bus and decides not to disturb Tina. She writes a letter of goodbye, and the chauffeur helps her load her things into the car. The streets are bustling as he drops her off at the bus station.

While walking towards the bus station, Paulette notices a red Corvette parked across the street. When Paulette gets to the window to buy her ticket, she's dismayed to find out that she had gotten the price for the ticket wrong. The ticket costs $30 over what Paulette was expecting, which means Paulette is short.

Paulette decides to head back to Tina's house. While she sits on the bench waiting for the bus, she notices that the red Corvette she spotted pulls up right in front of her. The driver rolls down the window and says "Hi." Paulette does not say anything. The driver says, "Now come on, I don't bite." He has a smooth friendly voice. Still, Paulette is silent. "Where you headed?" he asks. Paulette finally whispers "New York."

"My name is Peter, and I am on my way to the same place. Say, I have an idea. Why don't we ride together?" Paulette is thinking it over and Peter continues to pursuade her to come with him by telling her how great the trip will be. "We can stop from time to time and get some good eatin. I know of this place sells the best fried chicken." Paulette considers, thinking, *He does look hot. It would save me money. Money I might need for food.* Although Paulette's gut feeling tells her not to go with this guy, she is unnable to resist. The most pursuasive argument is that she's short on bus fare and will have none left over for anything else. Besides, Peter has some gorgeous eyes and a body to go with them. Paulette jumps in the car hoping she will soon be in New York. "Tell me, Paulette, how old are you?"

"Does that matter? I am old enough," she responds. There is a smirk on Peter's face that leaves Paulette feeling uncomfortable. "You know Pete"—she begins

"Peter is my name."

"Peter, you ask many questions."

"Just making small talk."

Paulette dozes off several times, forgetting how far Chicago is from New York. Peter does alot of stopping. She wakes up to see that this time, he is stopping in front of this gorgeous two-story home. "Say, where are we?" Paulette asks.

"You are home my sweets," Peter says jokingly. For the first time since she climbed in Peter's car, Paulette feels real apprehension. She responds, "This is not my grandmother's house. You said you would take me there."

"Oh, that plan was canceled," he says abruptly. At that moment, Paulette realizes she has made the worst mistake of her life. She begins to grab her things out of the car yelling, "Call me a taxi to take me the rest of the way." In a tough, threatening tone, Peter says, "Listen here, young woman, you're not going anywhere!" His voice sends chills down Paulette's spine. "Please mister let me go," Paulette begins to plead. I am only 16 years old. My grandmother is expecting me and will be worried if I don't show up."

Peter is unmoved by Paulette's cry. "Listen to you–you little twit, get your things and stop all that crying!" He holds her by the elbow and forcefully walks her up the driveway.

As Paulette enters the house, she notices several other girls sitting around. They look her age and some a little older. One girl, in particular, wears two long thick ponytails. Immediately they become friends. Paulette says, "My name is Paulette."

"Mine's Jane," the girl says. "That's a beautiful name," says Paulette and then asks, "What are all these people doing here?"

"You do not want to know." she looks away with a terrified expression. "Jane, please. I just turned 16. This guy is supposed to be taking me to my grandmother's house; please tell me what's going on."

"All right, I will tell you, but not until bedtime. You will be bunking with me." Then Jane rushes off to the other side of the room. *Something is not right here* Paulette thinks to herself.

But nothing further is revealed. They all sit down to dinner, and in a strange twist of irony, they have fried chicken, the one promise Peter has kept. Jane also keeps her promise at bed time to fill Paulette in about the house she has just entered. But she begins with her own story of how she got there. She tells Paulette how she was abused as a child and placed in a foster home. Then Peter came along and adopted her, and she has been living with him ever since. "Jane, why are all these other girls here?" Paulette asks. "Paulette he makes us do horrible things in this room." Jane keeps clearing her throat trying to hold back the tears.

"What kind of room?" Paulette asks. Both girls hear footsteps coming toward the door. Quickly they rush to their beds pretending to have been asleep. Jane whispers, "Paulette we have to be very careful not to make Peter mad. He does bed checks every night."

That evening, sleep does not come easy for Paulette. She is thinking of how she's gonna get out of this mess and if she will live to tell the story. "Paulette?"

"Yes, Jane."

"What did I do to deserve this?"

"Jane sometimes life is just not fair." Paulette closes her eyes, says a prayer, and drifts off to sleep.

On Wednesday morning, Paulette awakens just before dawn and knows she will soon have her answer as to why she is there in that house. Paulette begins walking towards a room that she feels may be the place Jane was talking about. She spots a bottle of wine sitting on the table. She hears music playing softly and sees a lovely gown nicely laid out on a bed. *What is this?* Paulette wonders. Suddenly, Peter's voice interrupts her thoughts. He takes the bottle of wine, pours a glass, and offers it to Paulette. Paulette refuses. Peter offers a second time, only this time it is clearly a demand, "Drink it." Paulette takes the glass. The wine is red in color and bitter in taste. Almost instantly, Paulette feels a little light headed. Then the room begins to spin. A man appears from nowhere and Paulette jumps. "Hey, don't be scared," the voice murmurs, "I won't hurt you." In the next moment, Paulette feels his breath on her neck. He is breathing heavily and she turns to look at him, taking an instinctive step back. The man is naked. He begins to tell Paulette how beautiful she looks. Paulette begins to blush. He asks Paulette to put on the gown. Giggling and stumbling, Paulette begins to get undressed. She drinks another glass of wine, and she remembers no more. For Paulette, the rest of the day is spent in the bed. Peter is very strict that the girls get plenty of rest. On the following morning, Paulette notices blood all over the gown. Frantically, Paulette wonders what to do. She begins to cry. "What's wrong?" Jane asks.

"Jane, I'm not a virgin anymore."

"Is that bad?" Jane asks.

"God wanted me to stay a virgin until I got married."

"Paulette, God still loves you."

"Jane, we can ask God to forgive us, and we will be all right, right?"

Paulette remains at the house for another year. She remembers more but she is numb to it. She creates a bond with the other girls. One morning, Paulette suspects she has missed her period. "Jane, I have to talk to you."

"Can it wait? I am busy."

"No!" Jane was always eating, and she loved to talk with her mouth full.

"You call this busy? Eating a donut?"

"Yes."

"Please?"

"All right, this best be important."

Paulette and Jane both run upstairs and close the bedroom door. "Jane, my period did not come."

"Oh, don't worry, it will. I read that sometimes if you are under stress, it doesn't come."

"Jane, stop and think for a minute. What if I am?"

"Then I say let's get to packing. We are out of here!"

Paulette slumps on the bed as she thinks about what this means. She shakes her head many times thinking, *When I need Jane's support she seems always to be joshing around.* Then Jane says sympathetically, "Paulette wait for 1 month. That way we'll be sure. We don't want to become homeless for no reason."

Paulette waits for another month, and there is no sign of a period. Around 8 o'clock the next morning, there is a knock on the girls' door. It's Peter, looking confused. Peter walks over to Paulette and he begins to talk to her about how he has noticed she is gaining weight. Jane rushes out the room.

Paulette tries to explain that she has been eating more than usual. Peter, looking puzzled, says, "Yes, this could be true, but to be on the safe side, I want you to take a pregnancy test." Paulette's heart starts to beat fast. She asks, "What for?"

"Well with you girls, you just never know." Peter shoves the pregnancy test in her hand and demands that Paulette take it. While reaching for the box, Paulette almost drops it. Paulette's hands are trembling. Paulette wonders whether Peter can tell how nervous she is. It took no time to realize the truth. The test is positive. A few minutes later, there's a knock on the door. It's Peter and he says, "Tell me girl you are not what we think you are." Before Paulette can say a word, Jane interrupts and blurts out the news that Paulette is indeed pregnant. Paulette has no idea what will happen next, and is somewhat surprised when she hears Peter say, "Paulette I am sorry to have to do this, but rules are rules." He walks towards the door, turns towards Paulette, and says, "Be out by tomorrow morning and forget you ever knew of this place. And with an expression full of menace, he threatens, "and remember this, if you cause trouble for me, I will find you." Paulette does not doubt Peter will carry through on his threat. She vows she will never tell anyone about this place.

Paulette begins walking slowly towards her bedroom, crying all the way. Paulette's eyes are blurred with tears as she fumbles around the room trying to get her things together. Suddenly she hears footsteps running up the stairs towards the bedroom. Jane enters the room gasping for breath as she tries to find out from Paulette what happened. Paulette begins to explain, and after she finishes, Jane begs Paulette to take her with her. Paulette begins to shake her head. She doesn't want to cross Peter. She feels for Jane but she knows this is not a good idea and says so. But Jane is frantic. "Paulette don't leave me here. Please. Listen, Paulette, for a whole year we have been together and we've built a friendship through all this madness. Paulette, you have to take me with you. What am I going to do without you?" This plea reaches Paulette's heart and she agrees. Both girls begin packing their belongings.

As they get their belongings together, Jane assures Paulette that she will not be in the way. She will not eat up everything. She will be good. "Jane, I should not be taking you with me. Peter is your parent"— Jane breaks in, her voiced raised in nearly a yell, "He is not my parent!" Jane turns to Paulette with tears in both eyes, "How can you say that? You see what goes on here."

"Fine. Get your things ready. We are out of here early morning."

"How early?"

"How about 6?"

"What about breakfast?" Jane asks. Paulette feels herself getting frustrated. "Jane either you are coming with me or not." With so much on Paulette's mind, she can't sleep. Jane on the other hand sleeps like a baby. "What I would give for rest," Paulette whispers to herself. Paulette realizes Jane is right about breakfast; she is eating for two. Paulette rushs downstairs and gets milk, cereal, fruit, bowls, and whatever else she can grab. Before she can run upstairs, the kitchen light comes on.

"What do we have here?" It's Peter's voice.

Paulette can't answer. Startled, she drops the bowls. "You can keep what you have, but if you ever tell a soul about me you will regret it for the rest of your life. Is that understood?" Paulette feels so scared she almost wets her pants. Paulette rushs past Peter so fast she almost loses her balance. By the time Paulette finishs taking a shower, Jane is awake. "Paulette is everything okay?"

"Yes, everything is fine. We have to get ready to get out of here. Make sure you have all your things."

Jane and Paulette pack all they possess and rush out of the house.

Chapter 2: Journey to Grandmother's House

Jane is happy to know there is breakfast. Paulette always seems to be thinking about something. "Paulette?"

"Yes, Jane."

"Where are we and how do we get to your grandmothers?" Paulette can't process her thoughts fast enough to respond when suddenly a blue car drives slowly past. Jane and Paulette turn and look at each other. "Are you thinking what I am thinking?" Paulette turns and looks at Jane and says "Do not even think about it."

"Come on, we are God knows where, what do we have to lose?"

"How about our lives?" Paulette answers. Jane turns to Paulette and tells her to stay where she is while she approaches the car. With a fierce look in her eyes Paulette tells Jane she is going with her. Jane begins to yell and whistle for the car to stop. The car stops and the girls see a little old lady sitting behind the wheel with a black hat on that looks old as she does. Her face is so wrinkled they can barely see her eyes. Jane says, "Hello Miss, sorry to bug you, but can you tell me where the nearest bus station located?"

"Where's yall headed?" the lady asks.

"We're going to my grandmother's house in New York, New York." The little old lady looks stunned and then asks the girls where they've been. She says, "Don't you know that is where you are?"

Paulette and Jane just look at each other and the lady asks,

"If Y'all like I could give Y'all a ride to the other side. Whereabouts do ya grandma live?" Before Paulette can answer Jane is already climbing into the car. Ms. Gretchen is her name, and she rambles on and on about grandchildren and her exhusbands. She just goes on and on. Finally, the car stops, and Paulette thinks, *Thank goodness!* Ms. Gretchen tells them that this is where their ways part but here's a bus stop. Then she adds, "You know Y'all shouldn't be takin rides from strangers." The girls thank Ms. Gretchen for her advice as they get out of the car. While exiting the car, Paulette turns to Jane and asks her to help find a pay phone. "There has to be one around somewhere." Paulette notices Jane staring across the street.

"Jane! What are you looking at?" Paulette follows Jane's gaze and sees a black Corvette parked across the street and a guy gesturing for her to come over. "Don't even think about it," Paulette tells Jane. But Jane simply motions to Paulette, "Come on we got this far. Let's just say Hi," and before Paulette can respond she crosses the street. Paulette yells out to Jane, "I am going to use the phone and will meet you back at the bus stop. See you when you get back." Almost across the street, Jane yells back "Deal" and runs as fast as she can across the street." By the time Paulette gets off the phone, Jane is pulling up in the Corvette. Jane introduces Paulette to James who has volunteered to take them where they want to go. Paulette feels she will regret giving into Jane's desire to go with this man, but as she looks at Jane's pleading face, she doesn't ask any questions. She just gets in the car.

Why do I let Jane get me into these situations? Paulette thinks to herself. Paulette tries to reassure herself that they are on their way to her grandmothers, but Paulette senses that once again they are in trouble. As they continue riding, there is silence for about 10 minutes. Paulette finally says, "So Mister James–"

"Just call me James," he responds.

"Well, James," Paulette continues, "Do you pick-up young girls all the time?" Paulette feels Jane's elbow in the side.

"Not often. You girls looked like you were lost, so I thought I'd come to your rescue." Paulette can tell they're getting close to her grandmother's house. But then nothing seems to change as traffic worsens. It's summer in the city. Children are running around fire hydrants and loud noises seem to come from everywhere. Before James can stop the car, Paulette jumps out and runs as fast as she can to greet her grandmother. Even though Paulette's grandmother is not expecting her, she recognizes Paulette. They hug, while crying and jumping up and down. When Jane walks up and says, "Hello, I have heard so much about you."

"You girls come on in. Paulette we have much catching up to do!" Paulette stops laughing and thinks *that is what I don't want to do*. Paulette's room still looks the same—like nobody has slept in this room since she lived here when she was 10. Jane says, "Paulette your grandmother is kind. What is she doing with such a huge house?"

"Well, everybody is grown now, and Grandpa died about 2 years ago, so I don't know."

"Do you think she will mind if I stay here with you for a while?"

"My grandma is right people as long as you either get a job, go to school, and stay out of trouble." Silence hangs in the air. Paulette looks over at Jane then says, "I am 16 years old and pregnant. How am I going to tell my grandmother?"

"Doesn't God work in mysterious ways?" asks Jane. From Jane's response, Paulette can tell Jane has not read much of the Bible, but she understands that Jane is trying to support her. "Jane, just think, if I had not gotten pregnant we would still be at that house doing God knows what," Paulette says. At that moment, her grandmother enters the room, which helps to change the subject.

"Child," her grandmother says, "Let me take a look at cha. Boy, you sure have gained weight. Tell me how everybody's doing and why did it take you so long to get here? You just kept calling, and your mama's phone is disconnected, but whatever was going on, I am glad you are here now." She leans over and kisses Paulette's forehead. "What would Y'all like for lunch?"

Jane's eyes light up. She feels like she hasn't eaten for days. Grandma fixes a couple of sandwiches, with Paulette's favorite grape Kool-aid. "Where's Unc?" asks Paulette.

"Oh, you know your Uncle. He never can keep still. Who knows what he is up to. Girls, make yourselves at home. I'm just gonna go upstairs to make sure everything is okay. It's been awhile since I had company and you girls look like you could use a good night's sleep." As soon as Grandma leaves the room, Paulette cannot wait to ask Jane about James. "Well?" Paulette gestures.

"Well, what?" Jane responds.

"Did you get his number?" Paulette asks.

"I thought you weren't interested in meeting any guys;" she waves the paper with the number in Paulette's face, and as she does so, she smells the scent on her own hand. "Wow, Paulette! James shook my hand, and his cologne still lingers on. Gosh, he is one hunk."

"Yea, a hunk that is too old for you." Paulette responds.

"Oh, lighten up mother. Just got a number not a date," Jane says. Jane and Paulette are the same age, but Jane seems pretty grown-up. After tidying up the bedroom upstairs, Grandma enters the room and lays on the couch. Paulette can tell by how she looks that she is not feeling too well. Jane and Paulette start walking towards the stairs. Before they can make it to the top, Unc jumps out from the landing and startles them both. Paulette is so happy to see him that she begins to cry. Paulette holds him as if she is holding on for dear life. Unc looks down at her and holds her tighter. Paulette introduces Jane and before Unc can ask any questions, Paulette tells him they'll talk later.

Paulette's grandmother lives on the west side of town. Not too much went on there, but it was enough to kind of make you wish you lived somewhere else. That night Grandma fixes Paulette's favorite meal, spaghetti and fried chicken. As Paulette wolfs it down, her grandmother admonishes her, "Child takes your time. You act like you eating for two." Paulette shakes her head and keeps right on eating. After dinner, Jane and Paulette dress real warm to sit out on the porch. Although there is a chill in the air, the night is pretty clear. For some reason, Jane is pretty quiet.

"Say, are you all right? Paulette asks.

"Yeah. She pauses, reflective. "I just wish I had my family. You know, do family things." Jane responds.

"Oh Jane. You do have a family, I'm family." Paulette then thinks to ask, "Did you call James?" Jane's eyes sparkle in the dark before answering. "No. Think I'll give him a call in the morning. Getting pretty sleepy." That night Jane tells her stuff about her that Paulette would never have guessed. Like that Jane's dad's white, and her mother's black. Jane says, "He left when I was only 2 months old." Jane says her mother became very ill and then passed on." Jane then had no family, and that's how she ended up with Peter. Paulette gives Jane a big hug and whispers in her ear, "God loves you. Things are going to be all right." While talking, Paulette's shares how she wants to be a doctor so she can make her grandmother better. Paulette hears the screen door squeak open. Grandma waves her hand gesturing for the girls to come inside. Jane sleeps on the top bunk and Paulette on the bottom. "Bunk beds sure do come in handy," Paulette says to Jane. "Pleasant dreams, Paulette," Jane says.

The next morning, Paulette awakens and she is not feeling well. Outside it looks as though snow is trying to turn to drizzle, but that could not be, because it's still August. She realizes that summer is slowly disappearing and she hasn't really been able to see and feel it at all. Summer, like her girlhood, were fast fading.

Not too long after, at 8:30 a.m., Grandma knocks on Paulette's door to let her know breakfast is ready. Jane jumps out of the bed, washes up, and begins to head downstairs. Boy, Paulette thinks,

Jane is so busy trying to get to the food she doesn't even notice me or that I'm not feeling well. But Paulette doesn't even have time to finish the thought before Jane pops her head back in the door, saying, "What's wrong? You look like death."

"That's a beautiful thing to say," Paulette responds. "Sorry" says Jane. "But don't you think you should tell your grandmother?"

"Jane, she can't handle this type of news. My grandfather always told me to be the best, and this is what I turns out to be." Jane walks closer to Paulette and grabs her hand. "Look, Paulette, either you tell her, or I will. You need some medical attention." Paulette sighs and turns her head towards the window. "Remember what I said," says Jane before rushing down the stairs. Paulette gets out of bed, looks in the mirror, and she notices her boobs are getting bigger. "Boy if Tina could see me now," Paulette thinks aloud. *No. On second thought. What would she think of me?*

Around 10 that morning Paulette decides to wash up and go downstairs. In the kitchen, Unc is cleaning up and Paulette plops in the chair right in front of him. Unc asks, "Do you want to talk about it?"

"Not really. Any more food left?"

"Just enough for you. And that girl–What's her name?" Paulette answers, "Jane."

"Yea, Jane. She can sure put away some food."

"By the way, where is she?" asks Paulette. Unc looks over and gestures to the phone, saying, "She's been on it for half an hour." *Who on earth could she be talking to?* Paulette wonders. Then Paulette remembers James. She has to be talking to James. Yep! She sees the look on Jane's face as she twirls the ends of her ponytails. Just as Paulette walks in, Jane is saying goodbye. "Guess what?" Jane asks. Before Paulette could take a guess, she informs Paulette that James is going to stop by to show them New York. "Jane," Paulette responds, "I don't think that is a good idea. What if this guy is married or something?"

"Paulette, you worry too much. You still has not taken any of my advice. Live a little!"

"We have been through hell and back and you say live a little Jane?"

"Listen, Paulette, my life has not been that happy, but I am not going to go around living miserable for the rest of it. If you're coming along, he will be here no later than noon."

"Jane I don't know why I let you talk me into these situations."

"Well?"

"Well, what Jane."

"Are you going?" Jane asks.

"Yes, can you give me some time to get dressed? Anyway is he going to bring a friend?" Paulette asks.

"That's a real question. We'll find out won't we?"

"Have you forgotten that I am with child Jane?" Paulette blurts out.

"Nope," Jane replies.

"Then why are you so insensitive to me?" Paulette wonders.

"All right what do you want me to do Paulette?"

Paulette walks away, confused as ever. She decides to stay home. She's not feeling well anyway. Jane continues to get ready singing softly to herself. James arrives exactly at 12 noon. Paulette cannot help but think to herself, *Boy, very impressive.* After Jane leaves, Paulette notices she is home alone with Grandma. A peaceful feeling comes over her. She begins to feel like this is her chance to share what has been going on in her life.

Knowing that Grandma is in her room resting, Paulette knocks on her door. Grandma calls out, "Come on in child, the door is open." Paulette wanders towards the bed, asking "How are you feeling this morning?

"As good as can be expected! Grandma is getting old. These bones just don't want to move sometimes." Grandma grabs Paulette's hand then says, "I know you didn't come in here to talk about me."

"You're right Grandma." Paulette replies and before she even seats herself on the bed she blurts out, "I'm pregnant."

"You're what?" Grandma responds, and then catches herself and asks, "I mean how—when did this happen? Child the minute I laid eyes on you I knew something was wrong. What happened and where is that momma of yours?" Grandma asks a flood of questions leaving Paulette without words.

Paulette notices that her grandmother's face tightens and she is holding her fist in a clenched position. Paulette breaks down and begins to cry as she tells her grandmother everything. "I told Gladys to leave that no good bum alone!" Grandma starts to cry as she holds Paulette tightly in her arms. She cries,"Child, why did you wait so long to call Grandma? Paulette the first thing we are going to do is go to the police and we're going to tell them everything, you hear?"

Paulette pulls away from her grandmother and tells her her fears about telling anyone. "He threatened to harm my family and me if I ever told." Paulette feels a little dizzy. The next thing she is aware of she's waking up to a doctor standing over her checking her eyes. Looking confused Paulette asks the doctor "What happened?"

"I am afraid you passed out," the doctor responds. "You need plenty of bed rest." A few hours later, Paulette is on her way home with instructions to stay in bed and take care of herself for at least a month. Paulette is happy to be going home. And she's even happier she told her grandma what happened. She has unburdened herself and she feels much better. However, she's still a bit drowsy, so she decides to go to bed.

Around 1 in the morning Paulette awakens to footsteps coming towards the bedroom door. Jane stumbles in. No words are exchanged and Paulette drifts back off to sleep.

Paulette spends time resting and reflecting on her life. She is happy that all she needs to worry about is taking care of herself and her baby now that she has a home with Grandma. But she does worry about Jane being so enchanted by James, who seems to be sweeping her off her feet. Paulette doesn't feel good about it, and Jane has been able to think and talk about little else. But the moment she tries to temper Jane's enthusiasm, Jane gets mad because from her point of view this is the first time in her life she's had a chance to be happy.

One morning, Paulette is awakened by the sun. It's beaming down on her face with such warmth and brightness that her eyelids are filled with light. The phone begins to ring and Paulette answers. It's Tina! Paulette can barely catch her breath she is so happy to hear from Tina. "What happened to you?" Paulette asks."I called and left you my grandma's number several weeks ago."

"Same old Paulette. Isn't you going to ask how I've been?" Tina replies, "and you could have called me again you know."

"Tina, I am glad you called back. You had me worried. Tina, you can't believe all that happened since I've seen you." As Paulette continues talking, she hears Jane stirring. Jane makes a deafening yawn and says "Good morning." Paulette continues talking until Jane butts in asking whose on the phone. Tina apparently hears her and blurts out, "You didn't tell me you had a sister!"

"I don't. That's my friend Jane."

"You had time to meet new friends? And you couldn't keep in touch with the old one?" Before Paulette can respond Tina quickly gets off the phone. Paulette hears the school bell sound in the background along with Tina's last words. "School!" Paulette repeats to herself. She hasn't thought about school in a long time. She turns to Jane: "Hello, Miss Jane." From the way Paulette calls her name Jane knows she's not pleased with her coming in the house so late again.

"Paulette before you start, I don't want to hear any of your lectures. I apologize for coming in so late. It will not happen again. You know how time flies when you're having fun! Paulette, promise–It won't happen again." This Jane has said before, and from the look in Jane's eyes Paulette know she's going to hear it again and real soon. Paulette shakes her head thinking to herself that Jane seems to enjoy living on the edge. As to Tina, she's a hyper young lady who appears to thrive off of attention. Jane and Tina are so different from Paulette, who is calm, not to mention pretty, quiet, and level-headed, at least most of the time. Paulette asks, "Jane if you don't mind me asking how old is this guy James?"

"He is 25."

"Do you know he could get in big trouble if certain people found out he was with you?"

"With me? Paulette, we are just friends. What's with you? I just turned 17 remember? My mother is not around and neither is my father."

"They may not be, but your friend is," Paulette replies. Jane, walks over to Paulette and says, "You know what you need?"

"No, but I am sure you will tell me," Paulette responds.

"Why don't you come and hang out with us at the park this afternoon?" Paulette looks out the window and answers, "I'll pass."

"Please?" Jane asks. Whenever Jane wants Paulette to do something she will give her a sad look. Paulette agrees but adds that she'll go to the park "just for a bit." Around 2, James picks the girls up, only this time he is in a Black Mercedes. Paulette nudges Jane and whispers, "What does this guy do?" Jane looks over at Paulette and mumbles through her teeth, "Who cares?" seemingly exasperated with Paulette.

When at the park, for the first time in a while, Paulette feels like a little kid. James chases them around the tree, Paulette goes down the slide and swings on the swing. Paulette is so busy having fun she forgets she's pregnant. She decides to sit and rest. Before taking the girls home, James takes them to this sweet spot for something to eat. Finally, James drops the girls off at home. From the time Jane gets out of the car until the time they step into the house all Paulette hears is "James this and James that." Paulette looks over at Jane and says, "Look, I know you had a good time and so did I. But are you really serious about this guy?"

"What's wrong Paulette? Are you jealous? Just worry about your own problems. By the way, have you told your grandmother about your child?"

"Don't think that it is any of your business, Jane." Then Paulette catches herself and says, "What are we doing Jane? Why are we arguing?"

Unc is sitting on the porch watching television. Paulette says hello as quickly as possible and rushes up to her room."Paulette," he calls up to her.

"Yes Unc?"

"Could you come here for a second?" Paulette takes a deep breath and proceeds down the stairs. "Have a seat." He then says, "Listen I was wondering about something."

"Yeah?"

"Well, I was wondering, would you like to take in a movie one day."

"Of course! When?"

"Is there something else you would like to talk about Paulette?"

"No? Just let me know," and Paulette proceeds to walk towards the stairs. She wishes she could open up and tell him what she's feeling. Upon entering the room, Paulette notices Jane getting dressed. "Just where do you think you're going?"

"If you should know, James is taking me to see a movie."

"You mean to tell me you're about to go out with him and he just dropped us off?"

"You thought I wasn't? Paulette, it's still early. The movie starts at 9:30 tonight. Look Paulette. For the last and final time, please minds your business."

"Jane I worry about you," Paulette replies.

"You know Paulette? That is your problem. You worry too much. I am a big girl. Relax."

James arrives, and Jane rushes out almost without saying goodbye. By the time Paulette gets out, "What time—" the door slams shut. Paulette cannot shake the feeling she has of foreboding about this and tries to figure out why is she bothered by a guy that neither of them knows. Jane is 17 now but Paulette thinks she is too young for this guy. But it's more than that. Paulette decides to turn in early for bed.

The next morning Paulette is awakened by a knock on the door. It's Jane. Paulette rushs to open the door asking Jane whether she knows what time it was. "Paulette not now! My head feels like a marching band!" Jane responds.

"Listen Jane, my grandmother and uncle are still sleeping so I could care less what's marching in your head."

"All right Paulette but can we talk about this in, let's say, 10 hours from now?" Jane walks off as Unc rushes down the stairs asking "Who's at the door?" He admonishes Paulette, telling her, "Paulette, you know your grandmother is not feeling her best these days and when is that girl going home?" Paulette thinks, *Unc always seems to make big deals out of everything.* At 6 ft. 2 with a long ponytail, he looks as though he never worked out a day in his life. "Paulette, don't you hear me talking to you? You know I don't like repeating myself."

"Oh, what were you saying Unc?" Unc shakes his head as he heads back toward his bedroom, still mumbling. Paulette notices her grandmother resting on her bed as she walks into her room. "Grandma, what are you doing up"?

"Grandma is worried about you. What about school and the baby?"

"Look, there's plenty of time to talk about that. Right now you need to get your rest," Paulette suggests while helping her grandmother to the bed. Her grandmother says, "Paulette, I am not sure what's going on with my daughter, but we need to go to the police and let them handle what has happened to you."

"Grandma you promised! Please! God is going to help me get through this." Slowly Grandma gets up and she says not another word. She strolls towards her bathroom. Paulette sits and watches as her 250-pound grandmother limps and hums her favorite song. *Grandma is right*, Paulette thinks. *Something has to be done but in due time.* Paulette sits rubbing her belly as she repeats the words to herself that help to soothe her. After spending much needed time with her grandmother, Paulette decides to turn in for the rest of the day, recalling her doctor's order to sleep.

One morning not long after, Paulette awakens to the smell of bacon and fresh hot biscuits. She notices that Jane's not home. Paulette walks over to the window. Taking a gentle stretch as she looks at the blue skies and the trees swaying softly she thinks how happy she is to be with her grandmother. Paulette freshens up and heads down the stairs to eat. Breakfast is delicious. While talking with Unc, the phone rings. It's Tina.

"Hey, girl what's happening with you?" Tina asks.

"Oh, me? Not much. Just trying to get ready to go to check out this continuation school around the corner," Paulette replies.

"Don't sound so excited Paulette." There were times Tina's sarcasm is not appreciated, and this is one of them. "Well, enough chit chatting," says Tina. "Paulette guess what?" Before Paulette can respond, Tina tells her that she will be visiting an uncle that lives here in the New York suburbs.

"Tina why?" Paulette is surprised at this news.

"Paulette, I hear where my uncle lives is a beautiful area not to mention I need different scenery." Paulette does not respond. Tina feels startled. Paulette always has something to say. She says, "Paulette something is going on, and you're not telling me."

"Not at all Tina, I am doing okay. When will you be here?"

"Sometime this weekend," Tina replies.

"Tina, your parents agree with you staying with your uncle?"

"Sure they're the ones that suggested it. I'll see you this weekend. Then we both can hang out." Tina says, "Gotta go, can't wait to see you!" and she rushs off the phone.

Jane comes home that evening around 8:30. Jane just jumps in the shower without a word. When Paulette hears a knock on the door, she opens it to Grandma, who asks Paulette, "How long does Jane plan on staying?" Paulette's answer is to shrug her shoulders and continue to get ready for the day. But Grandma does not let the question go unanswered. She lets Paulette know that she disapproves of Jane running in and out "like she pays the bills." Paulette looks over at her grandmother and says she'll talk to Jane to see what her plans are. Grandma continues to share a story about how she didn't allow Gladys, Paulette's mother, to behave like this ever. "Alright," Paulette replies, "You have said your piece. I will see what I can find out. But what if she has no place to go?"

"What do you mean?" asks Grandma. "Is she a runaway Paulette?" When Paulette does not answer, Grandma says in a no nonsense tone of voice that also says she cares, "Talk to me Paulette"

"Look grandma, I'm going to see what's going on, but we just can't throw her out on the streets. You taught me that God wants us to show love one to another, right?"

"Paulette, you have a week to get back to me. God says a lot of things." Grandma adds for good measure, "One week."

After Jane gets out of the shower, Paulette tells her they need to talk.

"About what?" Jane asks.

"Well for starters your living arrangements."

"What's there to talk about? I thought I would continue living here with you."

"Well, plans have changed. My grandmother is not pleased with the way you have been behaving."

"What do you mean?"

"How about you're only 17 years of age not to mention you're dating a guy that could be your father and–" Before Paulette can finish, Jane interjects, "OK, I admit that I have been not acting too appropriately. I will do better. Besides, where would I go? You can't just throw me out on the streets." Jane suddenly sees the predicament she's in and begins to cry hysterically. Paulette begins to shake her hard until Paulette has to give her a swift slap.

"Jane get ahold of yourself. We will figure something out. In the meantime, you have got to behave yourself. By the way, a good friend of mine will be coming to live with her uncle this school year. Her name is Tina. By the way, you just got out of the shower. Do you plan on going out again?"

"Well, let's see Mother. I don't know– Will it be all right with you if I just go to bed?"

"Very funny. We can talk later. You look drained. But have you thought about what you're doing with this guy?"

"OK, Paulette. The truth is James is picking me up later tonight if you don't mind. Paulette, I promise to do better after this one last time." Paulette doesn't respond. She just shuts the door behind her as she walks out, goes downstairs, grabs her coat and warm slippers, and steps outside to sit on the porch. It's mid-September, and the sky is clear. People are still hanging out in the streets. It's a little chilly, but the way Paulette is feeling, it helps to cool her down. *Time is going by fast* she thinks as she rubs her belly. It's actually growing. Paulette begins to smile as she feels a little flutter and quickly runs into the house full of excitement.

"Grandma, Grandma I felt something." Between catching her breath while trying to explain, Grandma finally catches on to what she is attempting to say. "That is beautiful, child! Look, you needs to get all your rest. Now just go and lay down. I'll fix you some good old hot chocolate. My great grand baby!" Paulette could see the happiness in her grandmother's eyes. That night James does not show, and Jane sleeps until 12:15 Friday afternoon. The next morning Paulette and Jane do not speak. Paulette takes a shower, gets dressed, eats and sits out on the porch. She then asks Jane if she wants to go out to the back and sit on the swing that her uncle made her when she was 5 years old. Jane nods. While walking, Paulette asks, "What's wrong?"

"Oh, nothing. I can't believe he didn't come over like he said he would."

" Well you know, it's not the end of the world. You're probably better off."

"You know you're probably right," Jane says, "but I like him. He makes me feel alive, and he buys me whatever I want. He treats me right." While she's talking, Paulette notices a mark on her chin looking blue in color. "Jane what happened to your chin"?

"What are you talking about?

"You know!"

 "Not unless you tell me."

Paulette doesn't want to talk about it and changes the subject."You know Jane, we were becoming close till this guy came along."

"Paulette let's talk about something else. He is history as far as I am concerned. He stood me up. Say why don't we get dressed and check out a movie?"

"That sounds nice, but not today, some other time. Not to mention the problem of no money."

"Paulette the movie is my treat."

"Jane maybe another time." Jane does not say another word but runs upstairs to the room. Paulette can think of nothing to say to make her feel better. She takes a deep breath and begins to walk. She stares off into the cold blue-filled sky. On the street, people are walking and talking as if the sun is faithfully shining. Then Paulette notices something rather odd. There's a black Corvette parked on the opposite side of the street not too far from where she is. "No. That can't be!" Paulette whispers outloud, but sure enough, James is sitting and talking with some young girl, and he must have just told her something funny cause she laughs. *Now if I were to tell Jane this or try to show her, would she believe me? With the way things have been going, I doubt it very seriously.* Paulette notices before he pulls off that the girl handed him a brown bag.

Chapter 3: Friendship and its Delimas

Paulette looks on as her mouth hangs open. She begins shaking her head and mumbles to herself that she has to tell Jane. She can't wait to tell Jane what she saw. Running as quickly as she can, she calls out for Jane. With disappointment written all over her face, she notices Jane is not there. For the rest of the day, Paulette sits and watches television while stuffing her face with ice cream. Suddenly, Paulette remembers Tina will be visiting on Friday. She decides to turn into bed early.

Around 7:00 in the morning the phone rings. Paulette ignores it.. When it continues to ring, she decides to answer and boy is she glad. It's Tina asking her for directions to her house. Tina arrives at 5:00 that Friday evening. Tina looks taller and thinner and she is wearing braces. Paulette just stands looking at her in awe.

"Are you just going to stand there or are you going to let me in?" Paulette shakes her head and invites her in. Tina is happy to see Paulette too, but cannot take her eyes away from her stomach.

"Yes, Tina, there is a baby in the bump. Pregnant, yes ma'am."

"You are what? How did this happen? Where is the baby's father? Paulette sorry for so many questions. It's just of all people I never thought it could happen to you! So besides being very pregnant, how have you been?"

"Me? Fine. What about yourself?"

"Considering I am moving here, pretty okay."

"Let's put your things away. We have much catching up to do." Paulette pauses, turns to Tina and says, "Before we go upstairs, there is something I have to tell you."

"Paulette, what is it?"

"My friend Jane who you heard on the phone. She's staying with me for a while."

"Wow, we do have some catching up to do," Tina responds. "Not to worry Paulette. A friend of yours is a friend of mine." *I am not sure about that* Paulette thinks to herself.

Paulette goes upstairs to make a place for Tina. Jane is still in bed and then the phone rings. When Paulette picks it up, James is on the other end. He asks if he can speak with Jane. Paulette wants to hang up the phone, but she also knows this call might ease Jane's pain. Gone is the urgency of telling Jane about James sitting in the car and being handed a brown bag from a girl. James picks Jane up later that evening around 8:30 and Tina and Paulette have an excellent time. They order pizza, eat potato chips, drink lots of sodas and eat candy bars.

"Paulette I have been waiting for a while now. Let's have it."

"Have what?"

"Who is this hunk that got you, you know!"

"Tina, that moment is something that I am trying to put behind me."

"Why? It couldn't have been that bad. A little pleasure is always satisfying."

In response to Tina's words, Paulette begins to cry.

"Hey did I say something wrong?" Tina asks. "We don't have to talk about it if you do not want to, but as your friend, I'd like you to tell me what happened." She adds, "Have you talked to anybody?"

"I told my grandmother bits and pieces but didn't go into detail about what went on. It's not something you want to remember." But that night Paulette tells Tina all the details of her harrowing kidnapping. Afterward, Paulette feels a bit better as they hug each other and cry. *Tina and Jane are so different* thinks Paulette. They are both her friends, but Paulette realizes the special bond she has with Tina. Tina says, "Paulette you have got to report this. If you do not, this guy is going to keep doing this to other girls."

"I know but right now is not the time. I am just glad to be alive. Don't worry, God will take care of him. Every evil person has their day."

"Just know that your friend Tina is behind you one hundred percent."

The baby is pretty active today and every time it moves Paulette feels a warm sensation run through her belly. The night finally comes to an end as Paulette and Tina prepare for bed.

Standing side by side washing up for bed, both girls look over at each other and smile. Tina and Paulette know each other well and are happy to be in each other's life again. Across the bed, head almost touching the floor, Tina is twirling her hair asking Paulette what she would like to be when she grows up.

"A doctor so that I could make my grandmother better."

"What about your friend Jane?" Paulette shakes her head and responds, smiling, "Jane is something else." She says, "You know ever since she met this James guy she has not been the same. Tina, don't get me wrong, he might be a good catch if you're old enough."

"What do you mean? how old is this guy?"

"Well, I am not sure. Jane says 25 but he could be in his late twenties."

"Well, you know what they say, age is just a number. I would like to meet this gentleman."

"I hardly think he's that. With about three or more cars and dressing in the finest gear, he has to be doing something else. I just don't know. Today I saw him talking to another girl younger than Jane."

"Did you tell her?"

"No, she was sobbing her eyes out. Enough talk about him. She is of age to know what she wants to do. My problems is big enough."

That morning, Jane stumbles in around 1 o'clock. Jane rushes into the restroom. Boy, *no Hello* Paulette thinks.

"Is everything all right?" she asks.

"Just fine. Be out in a minute." Tina looks at Paulette and continues to unpack. Jane finally comes out of the bathroom. "Paulette I had a great time." Jane stops abruptly as she sees Tina. "Oh I am sorry didn't know you had company."

Paulette responds, "This is no company. This is my dear friend Tina." Paulette lets Jane know that she wants to hear the rest of her story. Jane is rushing, talking fast, as she packs an overnight bag. James took her to dinner and on a shopping spree. She says, "He's waiting in the car. Help me get my bags out of the car."

"Gosh Jane, this guy sure is spending a lot of money! Are you certain he is legit?" Paulette asks.

"Don't be silly!" Jane responds as she pulls her bags from the car.

"Say, Paulette," says James, "I was wondering. Would you like to hang out with us Saturday night?" Then, on noticing Tina, asks, "By the way, who's the new friend?" Before Paulette can introduce them, Tina's hand is extended to James. "Tina is the name, and you must be James. It's pleasure to meet you. I've heard so many good things about you." While shaking his hand, Tina begins to think to herself, *what on earth does he see in Jane?* A brush on the shoulder from Jane interrupts Tina's thoughts.

"James is my new boyfriend," says Jane and Tina looks over at James.

"Honey hold this bag please; it's not light." James rushes over and grabs the bag from Tina and puts it on the porch. Paulette is astonished at Tina's behavior. All Paulette can think is *What have I started.* The next evening all three girls hang out with James and a couple of his friends. The whole time the girls are riding in his car Paulette notices James giving Tina the eye and she returns his advances. Paulette gives her a swift punch in the side. Tina looks over at Paulette, whispering "What did you do that for?"

"Listen James is Jane's man. Don't start anything."

"Oh loosen up Paulette! James is a big boy." Tina chuckles and then says, "James knows what's best for him." Paulette feels she has to do something to stop what's going on between these two. She turns to Jane and asks, "Jane has you thought about what school you will be going to this year?' As soon as she asks the question, Paulette feels like disappearing through the seat. *Why did I ask such a question?* Paulette thinks. *Stupid, stupid, stupid,* Paulette continues to berate herself. Jane doesn't respond. She acts as though she didn't hear Paulette. *Oh no! What if James doesn't even know how old Jane is?* Paulette feels a hot flash rush from her head to her toes. From that moment on Paulette sits riding quietly ignoring James and Tina's flirtations.

"Well ladies have you thought about what you would like to do this evening?" James asks. "Baby cakes you know my friends are waiting for me to call. Just say the word."

"Why are you asking Jane?" Paulette blurts out. Paulette taps Jane on the shoulder, saying, "I thought you told me this evening was already arranged." Paulette can see James is upset at hearing her response and he glances in his rearview mirror. But before Jane can answer, James breaks the silence: "How about I take you guys home since Miss smarty pants is having a bad evening?"

Soon after James makes his remark, he swerves through the intersection and the car feels like it's going to turn over. In less than 10 minutes, the girls are back home. Paulette seems to be the only one glad to be home. Paulette and Tina get out of the car and leave Jane to talk with him. "What a maniac! Did you see how he was driving?" Paulette says, unnerved by his recklessness. "He doesn't care if I am with child or not! What does she see in him?" Tina starts to answer and Paulette cuts her off, "Don't go there." After Tina and Paulette enter the house they can't resist peeking through the blinds at the scene they just left. But all they can capture is James yelling, Jane screaming, and James speeding off. Jane runs into the house to the room and slams the door. *Boy am I glad my grandmother is at church*, Paulette thinks to herself. Of course, Paulette and Tina run behind her. "Please go away!" says Jane.

"Jane, we are not trying to get into your business, but don't you think you are a little too young to be tripping with this guy?" Tina asks and Jane turns on her. "What does age have to do with anything, and who are you to come here and get in my business?" Tina looks straight into her eyes, "Look, little girl, you don't know anything about me." Paulette can tell the conversation is getting out of hand. While walking away, Tina turns and says, "Jane I am only concerned. Sorry for butting in, my bad." Tina then rushes downstairs. Paulette goes to Jane and says, "Listen we are only concerned."

"Paulette, you can talk to me anytime, but Miss whatever her name is has nothing to say to me about my business."

"Wow, Jane! I have never seen you get this mad! Maybe Tina was overstepping her boundaries, but—" Tina then enters the room sipping a coke cola, and Paulette says, "Listen to me girls. We are not even of age to be discussing this type of stuff. We are 17 years old and need to finish school. Right now we need each other, not some Joe Blow whom we don't even know. Please let's just try to get along. We all need each other." She adds, "My grandmother will be home soon, and she will not be in the mood for none of this foolishness."

"Foolishness!" Jane exclaims. "Is that what this is?"

"Allright maybe I used the wrong word, but you are smart enough to know what I mean Jane." Paulette feels a sharp pain rush down her lower stomach and immediately sit down and takes several deep breaths.

"Are you right?" Jane asks.

"I will be fine." Paulette sits and waits a moment to determine whether there's any more pain. Finally, she says, "It's been a long day. I'm going to turn in for the night. See you girls in the morning."

However, Paulette is unable to sleep that night. She finally decides to go downstairs where she has heard the television playing most of the evening. Unc is watching a movie and pigging out on pizza.

"Paulette what on earth are you doing up? It is past your bedtime."

"Unc I couldn't sleep."

"Why, you know your grandmother will be coming in soon, and she is already worried about you."

"I'll just tell her I wanted to stay up with you."

"Are we talking about the same grandma? Would you like some pizza?"

"Sure why not? A couple slices will not hurt. I have bigger problems than eating pizza."

"Look if you talking about that dizzy friend of yours Jane, she's a lost cause. One thing you will learn is you cannot save people. They have to want to be saved and besides there is a bigger problem to care about that you be carrying around everyday for as long as you live."

"You know Unc? You always know what to say."

"That's cause I'm your uncle." He reaches over and gives Paulette a big hug and kisses her on the forehead. The clock strikes 11:00 p..m. and Grandma is still not home from church. On her way upstairs, Paulette notices Jane coming down. "Just where do you think you are going?"

"James and I made up, so he is coming to pick me up."

"What happen to the long talks we had on respecting my grandmother's house?"

"Since when did you become my mother?"

"Jane, I'm not trying to tell you what to do, but this is my grandmother's house."

"Oh, I see. Well how about I grab my things and move out?"

"Don't try and twist this. You know what I am saying." Jane grabs some of her things before slamming the door, turning to

Paulette, and saying, "You have your friend Tina to deal with. I'm sure she'll keep you company." Jane storms out of the house and Paulette does not see or hear from her for 2 weeks.

One Saturday afternoon the phone rings and Jane is on the other end. Only this time, surprisingly, she wants to speak with Tina. Jane invites Tina to a party and arranges to pick her up that evening. Paulette cannot help but feel left out. She reflects that Tina doesn't seem ready to go to her uncle's house any time soon. Paulette knows she has to address this issue and says, "Tina, I know this is not the best time to talk about this, but don't you think your uncle is a bit worried about you?"

"Of course not, Paulette. It's nothing for you to worry about." Paulette stands beside Tina watching her as Tina gazes with satisfaction at the mirror, looking at her outfit from all angles, making sure her hair is intact. Paulette reflects on how great Tina looks. She's wearing some tight blue jeans with a half cropped sweater and her hair pulled back into a ponytail. There's a car horn sounding and before Paulette can tell her to have a good time Tina is heading out the door with barely a goodbye. Feeling like an afterthought, Paulette begins to feel sad. Unc walks over to her and says, "Paulette pull yourself together. You have a child to think about"

Paulette continues walking in deep thought as she proceeds up the stairs. She grabs a last glance at Tina as Tina jumps into a black Corvette, which drives off into the night. Paulette cannot stop wondering what James does for a living. *I do not believe he works*. Paulette remembers living in Chicago and a guy named Mark who drove several cars and wore plenty of gold, even in his front tooth. Everybody knew he was a drug dealer. There were times he would come over to the house and eat dinner.

Just as Paulette was getting comfortable, she hears a knock on the door. She rushes out of bed and runs downstairs. Opening the door, gasping for breath, she is sure Tina has returned. She opens the door and yells, "Tina!" in excitement. But before she can get out the rest she recognizes it is her mother who is standing there.

"Well, aren't you going to let me in?" But before Paulette can say anything, her mother walks on in. Before Paulette can run to get her uncle, her mother grabs her and tries to give Paulette a big hug. "Look at my little girl! Boy you sure have grown! Give Momma some sugar." Paulette turns her head and looks down on the floor before her mother can say more. She hears the key twist in the door and Grandma opening it. Grandma sees her mother and yells "Gladys" and Paulette can see that Grandma is happy to see her daughter. Paulette stands with a confused look on her face. *How could Grandma be pleased to see her after what she did to me*? Paulette wonders. Mama tries again to get Paulette to respond to her, "Just looks at my little pumpkin. Give mama some sugar."

"Mama," Paulette responds, "Let's see, you wouldn't happen to be the same lady that left me at the age of 15 to take care of myself now would you?"

"Listen here, girl! Don't talk to me like that! I still am yo mama."

"You still my mother. Well, I hope you found what you were looking for after y'all left me. Oh, by the way, I am soon to be a mother too or didn't you notice?" Paulette turns swiftly and goes to her room. Gladys simply turns to Grandma, a look of shock on her face. She starts to walk after Paulette and she bumps into Unc. "Say, you better watch where you're going" Paulette hears Unc say, "Who is this lady in my house? It cannot be baby sis?"

"Baby sis in the flesh."

"Listen you got lots of nerve coming here after that stunt you pulled leaving Paulette in Chicago alone! What happen?" Gladys sits down then begins to explain. "Charles, you don't understand! Living from day to day not knowing where your next meal is coming from is too much pressure."

"Mama told me how Chuck was strung out on that stuff. Why do you always cover for him?"

"I'm clean now and trying to get my life back on track. Yes it was wrong for me to leave my child, but I have a second chance, and that is what matters."

"Do you have a second chance?" Unc asks.

"Today I don't have that answer, but I am hoping to work things out with my little girl." Paulette feels overwhelmed with all that is already happening in her life. Now her mother! Tina returns that morning around 2:30, and Paulette is still up. Tina turns on the light to find Paulette sitting awake on the bed. "Hey, mom what are you doing still up? Its past your bedtime."

"My mother is here."

"What? Where is she staying?"

"Can you believe she showed her face here?"

"Paulette I think you should calm down. You have a child to think about, and the doctor said you need lots of rest."

"Look who's trying to give advice? You are so tipsy you'll probably forget what I'm telling you by morning."

"I am your friend whether tipsy or not. I know when danger is ahead. But you don't have to listen to me."

"I'm sorry. It's just so much has happened in the last couple of years. Tina, I have been through things that people older than us will never experience. My life feels like it was snatched away, and now I have more responsibility than any girl should have and that I didn't ask for." Tina grabs Paulette and gives her a big hug. Paulette begins to cry. Tina holds her as she strokes her back then says, "Just let it all out. I am here for you. God will make things better."

Paulette awakens around 9 a.m.. She walks over to the window with arms folded as she watches snow lightly sprinkle down from the pale grey sky. Paulette begins looking up towards the sky and softly whispers a prayer. "God if you can hear me, please help Jane to be all right. She is all alone in this big world. And help Tina and me in my situation. Amen."

Chapter 4: Paulette's Mother Returns (A Painful Moment)

Breakfast is in the air. Paulette gets herself together and brushes downstairs, only to find Unc is not cooking.

Paulette's mother is. Tina finally shows her face about 5 minutes after Paulette sits down.

"Good morning ladies," Gladys calls out. "Paulette, aren't you going to introduce me to your friend?" Paulette can feel her skin crawl as she fishes for words to say. Tina decides to introduce herself by saying, "Hi. I'm Tina. I went to school with Paulette in Chicago." Gladys looks at Paulette with a look of dismay. "Well, aren't you going to say something?" she asks. "Paulette, please join me for breakfast."

"Look if you are trying to make up to me, don't bother," Paulette says and runs upstairs. Tina stays and eats breakfast. She enters their room with a plate in her hand. "Look, friend, you have to eat something. My little godchild has to be healthy and active."

"Your godchild?" Paulette asks.

"That's right. He's going to need a beautiful woman like me in his life. Now eat up."

"Tina you couldn't have come at a better time. Thanks for being here for me." Paulette begins to tear up when all of a sudden she hears footsteps coming up the stairs towards her room. There's a knock on the door and Gladys calls out, "Tina, will you excuse us for a moment?" Tina looks over at Paulette to confirm it's okay to leave her alone. Paulette gives her a gesture that it's okay, and Tina leaves the room. Gladys enters and asks Paulette why she's not eating downstairs. "Unc is the one that always cooks breakfast," Paulette responds.

"Well, things change."

"Since when?" Paulette looks away and then says, "Oh, let me guess. Since you decided you want to become my mother again. Isn't that a beautiful picture to paint."

"Hey, I realize I made a mistake."

"A mistake? How about a disaster! Do you think you can leave me behind for a couple of years and then just pop back into my life like nothing happened? You've caused me so much pain." Tears begin to stream down Paulette's face. She says angrily, "Why did you come back? Never mind that question. When are you leaving? Listen, lady, I want nothing from you. Thanks to you, I'm pregnant."

"Thanks to me?" Gladys asks. "Look here missy, I'm not going to be blamed for your mishaps." Paulette leaps out of her bed and starts to walk out when suddenly she feels a sharp pain in her abdomen. *This pain is familiar* she thinks to herself. Gladys runs over to try to help. Paulette yells, "Don't touch me! Don't ever touch me!" Tina hears the commotion and runs upstairs as fast as she can.

Tina finds Paulette lying on the bedroom floor and yells out to Paulette. Then she turns to Gladys, asking, "What did you do to her?" Gladys opens her mouth as she starts to respond but then shakes her head and runs out of the room calling for Unc. Paulette is taken to the hospital. When she finally awakens she sees

Grandma's smiling face and tubes running all over her body. She asks, "What happen?"

"Now child, just get your rest. Grandma is here to take care of you now." Paulette notices Tina standing on the other side of her bed with a sad look in her eyes. Paulette then turns and looks at her grandmother to see a sad look on her face too. She says, "Come on guys, loosen up. Whatever happen, the baby and I are fine."

"Paulette. There's something you should know. The baby didn't make it," Grandma says.

"No! Grandma, please tell me what you're saying isn't true!" Paulette feels a rage of anger fuel her body and she starts shouting and screaming at the top of her lungs, crying at the same time. The nurse rushes in to try to calm her. The nurse puts everybody out of the room and gives Paulette a shot that causes her to sleep until late that night. Paulette is released from the hospital around 8:00 the next morning. Her thoughts are jumbled and disconcerting. She thinks about school, losing the baby, her mother, and life in general. The baby had been the one bright spot in her life. The loss seems more than she can handle right now.

Once in the car Paulette realizes Tina is not there and asks Grandma where she is. "Oh, she went to her uncles. School starts today." Paulette's head drops. She mumbles to herself, "I was supposed to start today. Unfortunately, I am confined to this wheelchair for the rest of the week. Losing a child is so painful." She stares out the window for the remainder of the ride home.

Upon entering the house, she notices how quiet it is. Paulette thinks, *That's strange. Gladys is always watching some television or listening to music. Wonder where she is?* As Unc helps Paulette up to her room, and Grandma goes to make Paulette some soup, Paulette sees her mother in her bed and says, "Boy, she thinks this is still her room. Just look at her."

"Now don't be that way, she's just getting some rest," Unc responds.

"Well, wake her up and tell her to go downstairs or somewhere." Unc begins to shake Gladys, but she doesn't move.

Paulette walks over and says, "Gladys this is my bed. You are not welcome in this room. Stop playing games." Unc notices something strange about her body. It's cold. "Paulette, this may sound crazy, but I think Gladys is dead."

"What? That cannot be? Pick her up! Shake her! Do something!" But Unc already is doing all he can. Unc notices a puncture on Gladys' arm and a tad of blood seeping out of it. Unc swiftly pushes Gladys arm away and tries to hurl Paulette out the room. "Paulette, we have got to tell Grandma."

"Unc, what did you see?" Paulette asks. Unc attempts to play dumb. "Why child I do not know what you are talking about."

"Don't lie to me. I saw you looking at her arm. Now tell me what you saw?"

"Paulette please! Child, you've been through enough! Now I must go tell your grandma the news."

"You go and tell her! I cannot face another thing." Paulette can hear Grandma screaming at the top of her lungs. "Lord, Lord my baby is gone," is all Paulette can hear her grandma saying. Unc calls the coroner. Around 3:00 that afternoon the phone rings, and when Paulette picks it up, she hears a man speak slowly on the other end saying the cause of her death was a drug overdose. Paulette drops the phone from her ear, runs to her Uncle screaming as she cries: "Why didn't you tell me?" Unc scratchs his head, asking, "Child what are you talking about?"

"You knew why my mother died! Why didn't you say anything?"

"Paulette I didn't want to give you any more bad news. Haven't you been through enough?"

"I thought she had changed her ways," Unc said softly, his head down. "Baby sis," he shakes his head sorrowfully, "I would have tried to help you if you would have let me know."

"Oh, stop with the world of regret. She is gone, and it's entirely my fault!" Grandma, who's walking down the steps, hears Paulette's words and says, "Paulette, you had nothing to do with your mother's death! She chose her lifestyle and we're going to miss her, but you simply cannot blame yourself! You've been through enough!"

Paulette can tell from the expression on Grandma's face that she's trying to be strong for her. For the rest of the afternoon, Paulette lay in bed weeping and asking God why. *Why was my life to go this way? What did I do? Please take away the pain. I can't bear too much more of this.*

For 3 days, Paulette is bed ridden. On the fourth day, she can barely get out of bed to wash up for breakfast. *What's my reason for living? Seems everybody that I loved was taken away from me,* Grandma brings Paulette breakfast in bed, and not much is said. Paulette just looks at her grandmother, her eyes full of tears. The entire afternoon Paulette ignores several phone calls. Finally, she decides to take a shower and get dressed. Around 5 that evening, Unc knocks on her door. He says in a low voice, "Paulette, can I come in?"

"Sure."

"Listen, I have brought you some company and I think this will cheer you up. Now I know you don't want to talk to nobody, but child, I think this will do you some good." Paulette feels like maybe a little company would help. Unc introduces her to Travis, the son of one of the church members on the deacon board. Travis is tall, about 6 foot 1, with short curly hair and skin smooth as chocolate. Somewhat shyly, Paulette walks over to him and introduces herself, trying not to act too anxious. "Are you all right?" Travis asks. Paulette responds, "I'm fine. Maybe a little fatigued for whatever reason."

"Let me help you," he says as he walks her to the couch and helps her sit down. Paulette expects that he'll sit on the opposite couch, but instead, to her surprise, he sits next to her. He asks, "Have you started school?"

"Not as of yet. I haven't been feeling too well these days. What about yourself?"

"I started today. I go to Washington High. It's a pretty good school. You should check it out."

"How old are you?" Paulette asks.

"I'm 16. What about you?"

"The same, 17."

"Why did you want to meet me?" Paulette asks.

"Your uncle is a good friend of the family and he thought you needed a friend. I couldn't resist meeting such a beautiful niece."

"Stop. I am not! Bet you tell all the girls you meet the same line."

"What I am looking at is beauty! You cannot change how I feel." Paulette looks at him and sees he is smiling. She is too. He asks, "Do you go to church?"

"No. Not in a while," Paulette responds, "but I need to start going."

"Would you like to go with me one Sunday? Look, here's my number. When you are ready, give me a call."

"Leaving so soon?"

"Yeah. I have to be at work by 6:00 this evening."

"Where do you work?"

"Right down the street at the ice cream parlor."

"Ice cream in this weather?"

"You'd be surprised at how many people eat ice cream in this weather. Come down sometime and check it out."

"Travis, I will take you up on your offer one day." Before Paulette and Travis can finish saying their goodbyes the phone rings. It's Jane. As Travis is closing the door behind him, Paulette hears Jane say, "What's going on?"

"Look, what do you want Jane?"

"Did I call at a bad time?"

"Let's see, considering I lost my baby and my mother overdosed, I would say you called at the wrong time."

"I am sorry to hear that! Anything I can do?"

"Not really. Considering a true friend would never go for days without calling a good friend."

"My apologies. I know the way I handled it was not good, and I just didn't know what to say."

"That makes sense. It's good to hear your voice," says Paulette, softening toward her. "So where're you staying?"

"With James. He's letting me rent one of his rooms."

"Rent? Are you joking Jane?"

"No. Actually, I want to pay my way. But I called cause I wanted to see how you were and to see if you would like to go on a double date."

"With who? You know how I feel about that."

"Yeah, but you should get over that. You know, you just might have fun. What can it hurt? Don't you need to have fun?"

"How old is this guy?"

"Oh, Paulette age is just a number."

"Well how old is he then?"

"All right he is 25 years old. Are you happy?"

Paulette says, "I guess that's not too bad. He's not that much older. Okay I'll go."

"Great I will pick you up in about 20 minutes. Wear something nice, but sexy."

"What? I cannot be ready that fast."

"Sure. Okay. How about 6:30 then?" Before Paulette can say another word, she hears a click. Jane arrives that night around 6:45 p.m. Upon entering the car, Paulette tells Jane she's not feeling too well.

"That's fine," says James. We'll have you home at a decent hour. We're just going to dinner." Paulette notices Jane is sniffling.

"Are you allright Jane? You seem to have a terrible cold."

"Just getting over one," Jane says. Downtown New York is lit up from one corner to the next. People are playing music, shooting dice, and playing card games. Downtown is not a place to be, but with the guy she is with, Paulette is feeling pretty safe. However, her suspicion is still getting the best of her. *Why did they ask me to go out to dinner?*she wonders. The restaurant is called Le Lieu. Paulette always wanted to go there, but you had to have money to eat there. People are wearing beautiful suits, with silk ties. It reminds her of some Cotton Club. That evening, Mark, her date, picks up the tab. For the first time in a long time, Paulette is feeling pretty good. She returns home around 9:30 p.m. and Grandma is sitting in the living room watching television. "Hello," she says.

"Hi," Paulette responds.

"I'm not going to ask where you've been. Do you feel like talking?"

"No, not tonight. I'm feeling tired. Just going to turn in for the night." The look on Grandma's face was a worried one.

"Don't worry grandma. I'm a big girl. I can take care of myself." Paulette kisses her grandma on the cheek and runs off to bed. The next morning, Travis calls wanting to know if he can come over after school. Paulette gives him a lame excuse (she has made plans to go to lunch with Mark). Paulette seems to be recovering pretty quickly from losing both the baby and her mom. Mark picks Paulette up around 1 that afternoon. Before walking out the door, Unc asks Paulette when she's starting school. Paulette looks over her shoulder and says she needs a little more time to recover from things.

"Just remember, if you wait too much longer, you're not going to want to go back."

"Yeah, yeah, I will see you later. Don't wait up for me. I'm not sure when I'll get back."

"Paulette, who is this new guy you are going to lunch with?"

"What are you doing, spying on me? Look, I'm meeting new friends, and that's something you're just gonna have to get used to." Paulette slams the door behind her. The anger she feels is almost out of her control. She's angry, but she knows Unc is right.

However, as the days go by, Paulette finds herself hanging out with Jane and her crew more and more, and she doesn't go back to school. The girls Jane hang with are also kind of weird. But she dismisses the thought because she feels that she can stop the pain for a minute when she's with them. Or so it seems for now.

Chapter 5: Moving Beyond The Pain

Paulette cannot understand why some of Jane friends want to hang out on the corner, get into cars and come back. Paulette returns home and rushes to her room not wanting to talk to anybody. Once in her room, Paulette falls on the bed. As she flips her pillow, there's a phone number lying under her pillow. Why hasn't Paulette noticed it there before? Paulette decides to call the number. There's a code, so she gives it soon after the phone is answered. The voice on the other end sounds familiar and calls out Paulette's mother's name. No, it could not be. Then he calls out her mom's name again. Paulette drops the phone. Then she realizes he's still on the other end. She picks up the phone and says she dialed the wrong number.

That Wednesday Paulette decides to enroll in a continuation school to complete her education. The school has been in session for about 2 weeks. *Something weird is going on,* Paulette thinks. Paulette has not talked with Tina in a while. She knows they would be going to the same school, and Paulette hopes to speak with Tina soon. Tina's uncle lives not too far from Paulette. *That's funny*, Paulette thinks. Tina's uncle is Tina's father's eldest brother, and they live so differently. Paulette stops by the registration office to get a copy of her schedule. The first period has already started. Upon entering the class, Paulette notices Tina sitting in the front of the class. Tina beckons for Paulette to sit next to her. "Where have you been?" Tina asks, "You know I called and left several messages for you."

"Nowhere, just been hanging out with Jane and her crew." Paulette sighs with relief as they compare classes. They have all six classes together. This time in class together, it's such a thrill. And having a female teacher is exciting. The teacher's name is Ms. Pete. Ms. Pete had long brownish hair that touches her lower back. Her eye bulges out of her head, but she has a beautiful smile. Whenever she turnes to write on the board, students make fun of her. Paulette leans over and whispers to Tina, "I thought those days were over."

"I thought kids at continuation school were older, but I guess the kids at this school are not that much older after all." Tina says. Tina starts asking Paulette all these questions until the teacher has to come over and tell them they have to quiet down or they'll be excused. Before Tina can say anything, Paulette looks at her and whispers, "Let's talk after class." Tina looks at Paulette in silence and nods her head.

After school, Travis asks Paulette if he can walk her home. Paulette looks over at Tina. "Why are you staring at me? My uncle is picking me up. Well, I'll see you tomorrow. Go ahead. I'll be all right." Travis gives her a big smile, and Paulette knows by the look in his eyes that he wants to be more than just her friend.

As they walk, Paulette begins to shiver. She says, "Maybe we should've taken the bus instead of walking. It's pretty chilly."

"Are you alright?" Travis asks.

"I'm just a little cold." Travis then grabs his scarf and wraps it around Paulette's neck. "You know you have beautiful eyes, and he kisses Paulette on the forehead. Paulette feels as though firecrackers are going off all through her body. The cold seems to disappear. When they arrive at her house, Paulette kisses Travis on the cheek and runs towards the house. Travis yells to her, "Will I see you tomorrow?"

"Yes you will!" Paulette responds. After entering the house, all Paulette can think about is Travis and how nice he is. The phone rings, interrupting Paulette's thoughts. It's Mark. *What perfect timing*, Paulette thinks to herself. It's as if Paulette can't be alone with her thoughts for a moment. He says, "Hey gorgeous I was wondering if would you like to go out and join me for an early dinner?"

"Sure. What did you have in mind?" Then, Paulette pauses and says, "On the other hand, I better not. I have homework."

"Baby, listen I just bought a brand new Corvette and want to test it out."

"You what? Of course I want to go! What time will you be here?"

"About 7:00. Is that enough time for you to get yourself all dolled up for me?"

"You got it! See you at 7:00."

As Paulette gets ready for her date with Mark, she can't help but think about Travis. *What's going on?* She wonders. *How can I just drop Travis to go out with Mark like it's nothing?* Paulette hears her grandmother stirring around in her bedroom. Trying to avoid Grandma, Paulette runs right into her uncle.

"Just one-minute where do you think you're going?"

"Unc wish I could chitchat but I got to go. Don't wait up for me." Paulette finds herself saying this quite a bit. Whatever her momentary hesitation on behalf of her feelings for Travis, Paulette can hardly wait to jump in Mark's new Corvette. Before Paulette can close the door, Mark leans over and kisses her on her cheek. "Don't you look lovely, and that smell! What you are wearing?" Paulette says, "Something my mother gave me," but then Paulette starts to feel sick remembering all the times she lectured Jane about dating an older man. Now she's doing the same thing.

"Paulette," says Mark, "How'd you like to go to a party with me tonight?"

"Tonight? I have school tomorrow, and I need to get home pretty early."

"Listen sweety. We won't be at the party but a couple of hours I promise."

"You promise?"

"Scout's honor!" Mark replies. Paulette notices the gold that trims Mark's front teeth as it sparkles from the glare of the streetlights. The ride is short, and soon Paulette is surprised as Mark pulls up in front of this huge house with nothing but gorgeous cars in front. Paulette can't help but be impressed by all of this. Mark gets out of the car first and then walks over to Paulette's side to open the door. "Baby, we're here. You getting out?"

"Sure," Paulette responds bluntly. Before Paulette can enter the party, she's shocked to see Jane. Jane begins walking towards Paulette. Paulette notices how different Jane looks. Jane has on some tall heels, a short skirt, and lots of make-up. *Why is she dressed like that?* It's not like Jane's usual attire; the make up really thick, the heels an inch taller, the skirt barely below her butt. Jane says, "Come on Paulette, let me introduce you to some new girlfriends of mine."

"Different friends? Jane you make it sounds like they're your girls for hire."

"Oh Paulette! You need to loosen up." Then she smirks.

"Whose party is it?" asks Paulete.

"Paulette you were always one for questions. If you must know, it's my birthday."

"I didn't know it was your birthday!" but Jane doesn't respond to this and simply procedes to introduce Paulette to her friends. Paulette notices that one girl, in particular, has a black eye. "What happen to your eye?" Paulette asks.

"I fell and hit my head on the corner of my living room table."

"Oh," Paulette continues to walk around.

"Paulette is you thirsty?" asks Jane offering Paulette what looks like red punch, which Paulette sips on for the rest of the night. Paulette is having so much fun that she doesn't notice the time going by. Then she finds herself sitting in the living room almost alone. It seems like everybody's disappeared. Suddenly Paulette hears loud laughing and decides to follow the noise. Paulette walks upstairs and towards a closed door from which the noise is coming. As she begins to push it open, she sees Jane looking up at her, some white stuff on the tip of her nose. "Paulette!" screams Jane in surprise. "Come in. Since you're here, you might as well join in the fun." Jane hands Paulette a mirror with lines of white powder on it. When Paulette just looks at it, Jane says "Well?"

"Well, what?" asks Paulette.

"Look, Paulette, I know you didn't travel all the way up these stairs to see me. Here, live a little girl, take a hit!" At that moment, Paulette can hear Unc's voice telling her, "this crowd means you no good." Paulette pushes the mirror away and says, "Jane, where's Mark? I got to get home. Got to be heading to school in the morning." Seeing Jane's shrug, Paulette turns and rushes out of the room, saying "Chat with you tomorrow." As she leaves the room, Paulette can hear laughter and one girl say, "Don't worry about her. She's just scared. She'll be back,"

"What?" Paulette thought outloud. "Not in a million years." Paulette finds Mark and notices that he too has a mirror with some lines of white powder held up to his nose. *What is going on around here?* Paulette thinks. *What is so great about white powder?* Paulette begins shaking her head as she walks towards Mark. Mark looks up after taking a hit only to find Paulette standing in front of him. "Hey baby what're doing here? I thought you were out with some of the girls."

"Ya, I was, until I realized it is time for me to go home."

"Paulette baby, the party hasn't even started," Mark replies.

"Mark as far as I am concerned this party is over. I'll meet you out at the car. And wipe your nose. What is it with this white powder?" she yells as she leaves. Paulette sits in the car for at least

15 minutes. When Mark finally shows up, no words are exchanged for the entire way home. Then he says, "Paulette, please say something. Look I really thought you'd have a good time." Paulette responds, "I'm not sure what's going on back there, but it's not okay."

"What do you mean baby? Nothing is going on back at that house."

"Mark, what do you do for a living? I am not even sure Mark is your real name."

"Look I sell life insurance. I already told you baby."

"Mark I may be young but I'm not stupid. Those girls I met tonight looked like they are the product for sale."

"Paulette, I'm sorry about tonight. You know I wouldn't do anything to hurt you. Let me take you to get a bite to eat before I drop you off home."

Paulette likes what she hears. "That sounds like a winner! I am a bit hungry." As Mark starts driving towards downtown, Paulette is feeling okay again. She watches all the colored lights, hears the bustling of honking cars, people yelling and shouting, and they pass by prostitutes as they go downtown to where the best restaurants are. Paulette wants to go to Le Lieu again and that's where Mark takes her.

The next morning, Unc is fixing breakfast and asks, "Paulette, who is that new guy I saw drops you off last night?" She repeats what she told him last time he asked her that: "Unc, Are you spying on me again? Can't a girl have men friends?"

"Paulette, don't take it the wrong way. You've been through enough and I'm just looking out for you."

"Thanks, Unc, but I think I can take care of myself." Paulette feels like somebody is watching her every move and it's starting to get on her last nerve. She runs upstairs to get ready for school. The phone rings, and Paulette answers. Paulette doesn't end up going to school. Instead, she hangs out with Jane and her crew. The girls Jane hangs out with are dressed funny like Jane. Paulette tries smoking a cigarette and almost chokes to death, and it leaves a bad taste in her mouth. *How can people enjoy smoking?* Paulette has a few swigs of the bottle the girls pass around. Paulette returns home pretty out of it. Thank God her grandma's not home. However, Unc is sitting on the porch. "Girl you look a mess."

"Unc, please. I do not want to hear your lecture."

"Oh I am not going to say one word, but you need to stay away from that crowd. They mean you no good."

"Whatever," Paulette responds and walks in the house.

The phone ringing wakes Paulette out of her sleep. "Hello?"

"Hey, where have you been?"

"Who's this?"

"What's wrong? Can't you recognize your best friend's voice? Tina adds, "Why haven't you been to school?"

"Tina, please. Can I call you back? I need to lay down. Call you later," says Paulette. However, after hanging up the phone, Paulette decides she wants to fix herself a bite to eat and watch some television. Upon entering the living room, Paulette notices Grandma lying on the couch. Paulette tries to rush towards the kitchen without being seen.

"Just a minute Young one, I do think we need to talk." This was a lecture Paulette knew she could not ease her way out of.

"Baby girl, I know you have been through a lot, but please, baby please, why start drinking?"

"Grandma, what are you talking about?"

"Don't play dumb with me. What's this?" asks Grandma holding up a bottle.

"Where did you find that?"

"You tell me! Where you left it."

"That's not fair. I have no privacy around here." Paulette runs up to her room. Paulette cannot believe how her life is going, not to mention why. Paulette is furious because she has to get something to drink. She can hear her grandmother shuffling her feet as she walks up the stairs. She hears her bedroom door open and her grandmother walks in. "Grandma, are you going to start again?" asks Paulette. "Do I have to move just to get some peace around here?"

"Paulette, child, if that's what you feel you have to do. I'm only trying to help direct your life."

"Well, you sure have a funny way of showing it, being that when my mother was alive, you acted as though nothing happen.

"Paulette, child, is that what this is all about? You coming in the house all time of night, not going to school, and basically doing what you want to do? Listen, I am sure your mother suffered for what she did, and just for your information, I was going to ask her about it, but then she died. What was I to do? She was my daughter." Grandma begins to cry and Paulette feels sad, not to mention wanting a drink to help calm her nerves. Not only that, but Paulette knows her grandmother is pretty sick these days and Paulette is not helping. She's just adding more stress. She says, "Grandma I'm really sorry for the things I said. I guess I feel so empty, and I don't understand what is going on in my life."

"Precious, can I say one thing? That crowd you're starting to hang out with isn't helping the situation. You need to be around positive people. Where's Tina these days?"

"Grandma, I just want to for once enjoy my life. Please, can you let me do that?"

"Grandma is here if you ever need to talk, and I will always love you."

That night, the stars are shining bright and for some reason, Paulette senses that there is somebody watching over her. She decides to say a little prayer. "If there's anybody up there, please hear me. I can't understand why these things have happen to me, but please help me to be a better person and touch grandma's body. Amen!" This is not the first time Paulette has ever said a prayer but somehow it feels like the first. She actually feels something will happen. And it does.

That Thursday morning she awakens feeling really down. The thought of her baby being dead makes her feel so depressed and then she notices grandma isn't up. The house is kinda shafty and the wind is blowing quite hard. Paulette hears it whistling through the air. She calls out to Grandma to see if she would like the heat on but there's no response. When she calls again, Grandma finally answers. Paulette opens Grandma's door very softly and sees that Grandma is lying in bed evidently in lots of pain. "What's wrong?" Paulette asks. "Come sit beside me" Grandma replies. Paulette sits next to her. "Paulette, Grandma is sick. The doctor says I need to have my right leg removed." Tears begin to fill Paulette's eyes as Grandma shares the story. Grandma tries to reassure Paulette. "Listen there's no need for you to worry. Grandma is going to be alright. The doctor say they want to operate as soon as possible." Paulette says "No, you can't let them do that! You know what will happen. You just can't!" Paulette runs downstairs and begins to scream, swinging her fist in the air asking what she's done to deserve such a life. The urge to take a drink is so strong that Paulette simply can't resist. A glass of wine always calms her. Even though it's early, Paulette decides to call Tina. Tina doesn't answer so Paulette leaves a message. She can't help but think about what Unc told her about Grandma. Afer taking several more drinks, she whispers a prayer, goes to her room, and dozes off to sleep.

The next morning, Paulette starts to get ready for school and notices she has the worst hangover ever. She simply goes back to bed. After drifting off to sleep, she hears a knock on the front door. Paulette does not move. She hears the knock again. Paulette thinks, *Oh, it must be Travis. Well sorry but this girl just can't make it to class today.* At the third knock, Paulette begins to wonder, *Where is everybody? Looks like I'll just have to answer the door myself.* She asks from behind the door, "Who is it?"

"Tina."

"Girl, what are you doing here?"

"Aren't you going to school?"

"Not today, my eye is still messed up."

"Well, that's a good reason."

"Wait a minute. How did you know I wasn't going today?"

"Paulette. I'm your friend, remember? You sounded pretty wasted when you left that message."

"Enough of the joshing Tina! What happen to your eye, and I want the truth."

"Well, do you remember when I told you that I liked James? Well, I kind of started seeing him."

"What! After you knew he was seeing Jane? How could you do that?"

"Paulette she's your friend, not mine. Anyways, one day I said something he didn't like, and this is what I got."

"What did you tell your uncle?"

"Tell him what?"

"Girl, what do you mean what? Somebody has to put him in check."

"Paulette you don't understand. It really was my fault."

"I really don't want to continue this conversation, Tina. Jane is my friend and so are you, and what he did was wrong. You need to stop talking to this guy."

"Thanks for the advice but I have it under control."

"Don't say I didn't warn you! Anyways, I need to get back to bed. My head is hurting. Call me later." Paulette shuts the door thinking, *The weight of my world feels overwhelming.* She feels as though she's a spider tangled up in her own web. Paulette pops two aspirins and jumps back into bed. She thinks, *When will my life finally get back to normal? Then again, what is normal?* When Paulette awakens, she feels much better. She decides to take a shower and make herself some lunch. Grandma walks into the kitchen. "Oh, hi Grandma. Didn't hear you come in," Paulette says.

"Child what is on your mind?"

"There are just so many things that have gone on in my life and I wish I could understand it all," Paulette responds.

"Precious, remembers we don't ever know why things happen. We just have to pray and ask the man above to help us make it through whatever it is."

"Thanks for such comforting words, but I still feel confused."

"Well," says Grandma, "I can't change the way you feel. Why didn't you go to school today?"

"I have a few questions myself, like why didn't you tell me you had cancer?"

"Child, I didn't want to worry you. You have enough on your mind. Grandma is going to be alright."

There's a knock on the door interrupting their conversation. It's Travis. "Travis, what are you doing here?" asks Paulette. She adds, "Or better yet, why aren't you at school?"

"I haven't seen or heard from you since that day we walked home together, so I just wanted to make sure you were okay," Travis responds.

"That's very thoughtful of you. But as you can see I'm fine." Travis looks at Paulette with a look of concern. "Well since everything is alright here, I guess I'll be going."

"Wait!" Paulette shouts. "Would you like to have lunch with me?"

"Paulette I really have to get back to school."

"Please, you might as well. School is almost over. It will be in the next 3 hours." Travis lets out a big sigh. However, it doesn't take much for him to change his mind. The rest of the day they spend watching television and eating junk food. They laugh together and time goes by quickly. Travis looks at his watch and says, "Wow look at the time! I've got to be going. I got to get to work."

Unc comes home just in time to take Travis to work. The weather seems strange. At first it's drizzling, then it starts to pour down rain. Before walking up to her room, Paulette notices Grandma lying on the couch. "Hey, are you alright?"

"Grandma is doing fine. Just feeling a little tired from all the medicine I took."

"Just make sure you call me if you need anything you hear?"

"Precious, you worry too much. The man upstairs is watching over this old tinker."

"That's good to know, but this young Tinker is also watching." Paulette plops down on the bed. She thinks how it is already September 17th and wonders where the time has gone. She reflects outloud to herself, "What have I accomplished besides a drinking problem?" The phone interrupts these thoughts, but Paulette lets it ring. When she picks it up, she hears Jane's voice.

"Hey, girl what's up?"

"Jane!"

"The one and only."

"Where are you?"

"Well, I'm still alive and still in New York. Listen, the reason I called is because I really need to talk to you. Can I come by?"

"Of course. What time?"

"How about now?"

Chapter: 6 The Mystery of the Night

Jane arrives around 5 that evening looking pretty down.

"What's wrong?"

"James that scum. He's found another woman."

"What makes you think so?"

"It is just women's intuition."

"Jane do you have evidence that he is seeing someone else?"

"No!"

"Well don't judge him until you're sure."

It's hard for Paulette to keep eye contact with Jane. She's not good at deceiving her friends. She feels like she's caught in the midst of a whirlwind. *What should I do? Tell Jane that Tina is the other woman?* Paulette wonders.

"Paulette! Paulette! Are you listening to me?" Jane is shouting.

"Sure I heard everything you said." Paulette notices the whole time Jane talks Jane is sniffling.

"Well, Paulette, that is what I had to talk to you about. Why is he doing this to me?"

"Jane please don't worry. He's probably just busy working on something."

"Paulette do you know something I do not? You would tell me right?"

"Why would you ask a question like that?"

"We are friends and that is what friends do Paulette." Although Paulette feels their friendship is important, she just can't bring herself to tell Jane any bad news, friends or not. Although she never liked James, it seems there's not much she can do about Jane's choice in men. She feels like giving up trying. Jane doesn't press her. Jane then says, "Well, got to run. James is taking me to the movies tonight."

"Jane I thought you just told me—"

"I know what I said, but who could resist that guy's smile?" As Jane walks towards the door on the way out, Paulette notices Jane is getting rather thin. *She looks tired. What's going on with her?* she wonders. For the rest of the day, there isn't much to do. Paulette just sits staring out the kitchen window and continues to drink. All kinds of thoughts run through Paulette's head. *What am I going to do? Will I continue my education or become a loser? The answers I guess lie within.* She feels an emptiness inside like she's longing to be held and she decides to call Mark. He picks up the phone on the first ring. Paulette says, "Boy talk about fast! You been sitting by the phone?"

"That's right. Waiting for you to call, and I'm glad you did. Listen, I do apologize if I did anything to hurt you."

"Mark you didn't do nothing. It's just when I was at that party there was so much going on I didn't understand."

"Listen there's nothing for you to worry about. You are in great hands. Don't worry about other people and their problems. How about dinner?"

"What time will you pick me up?"

"About 7:30 p.m."

"That's only an hour away."

"Good, you know how to tell time." That evening Mark lets Paulette know how sorry he is. They have dinner, play video games, and even go to this club. Mark seems to know everybody, and all the guys want to talk to him. Paulette tries to understand how she got into the club since she was under age, but Mark has everything under control. That night Paulette returns home drunker than ever. She doesn't even remember getting home. The next morning Paulette awakens with another terrible headache. When in the kitchen, Grandma starts talking, and Paulette responds, "Grandma I don't know what you are talking about."

"Let me refresh your memory." By the time Grandma finishes talking, Paulette realizes she only remembers partial things about the night before. Grandma asks, "Child when are you going back to school? You have not been to school but 2 or 3 days. Please tell me what's happening with you?" Grandma begins to cry. She looks at Paulette with tears in her eyes, and Paulette asks, "Grandma, why do you weep?"

"I worked very hard so that you and your mom could have a better life. I could never get Gladys to see she could do better. Running off with your father at such a young age. Paulette, it is just not right. Now, I look at you, and you're traveling down that same path."

"Please don't say that. I know I haven't been doing what I should." Paulette grabs her Grandma, pulls her close, and hugs her as hard as she can. She whispers, "I will do better. I promise." Grandma looks Paulette in the face as she rubs the side of her face and responds, "Baby, I sure hope so." The wrinkles in her grandmother's face holds the tears she sheds as she turns and walks away. Paulette begins to feel sorry for putting her grandma through all this pain, and she vows that she will get herself together starting that day.

As Paulette begins to get in the shower, she notices there's a bruise on her thigh. She wonders how she got the bruise. While in the shower, Paulette begins to pray, asking God to help her get her life together. After taking a long shower, Paulette gets out singing one of her favorite gospel hymns. While Paulette is getting dressed, she notices there's some money hanging out of her jacket pocket. It's about $70.00, and it seems to have appeared overnight.

Paulette can't remember where she got the money. "Maybe if I talk to Mark he'll be able to help answer some of my questions," Paulette says aloud. She immediately reaches for the phone, but receives no response from Mark. She leaves a voice mail and continues to get dressed.

Saturday morning is always nice. Unc cooks a big breakfast and while eating they watch some television and talk about life. *My life of course,* thinks Paulette. "So my dearest Paulette, what's going on with you these days?"

"Unc, I don't know. I just have so much on my mind."

"Like what?"

"Well for starters I am messing up badly in school, and there are these two guys that I do like, but I know one of them is no good for me."

"What about the other?"

"Well, I know he is right for me."

"If you know that, what's the problem?"

Paulette chuckles, responding, "That's why I'm talking to you." She says, "Unc, I wish it were that easy, but it's not."

"Paulette, you have to make the right decisions for yourself and pray that you make the right one now. Right now Paulette, I think you are too young to be getting caught up with these boys. You have a long life ahead of you, and I think you should focus on school and pursuing your dreams." A knock on the door interrupts Unc's lecture for the day. Tina appears. "What are you doing here?" asks Paulette.

"Paulette I need to talk to you." Tina walks in, pulls Paulette by the hand, and they both rush up to Paulette's room. Tina is breathless as she tells Paulette, "James and I are getting married!"

"What? You can't do that!"

"Why not?"

"What about school? Or better yet, what about Jane?"

"I'm preparing to take my GED, and as far as Jane is concerned, that's your friend, not mine. I told you that! Paulette, I am telling you because I want you to be happy for me."

"How can I be happy for you when I know you are making a terrible mistake?"

"What have you got against James."

"Tina what happen to all the dreams we use to sit and talk about?"

"Paulette all I want is your blessing as a friend."

"Tina I cannot do that. You need to think this through. Do you think he loves you?" Tina just looks at her, and Paulette says, "How do you think this is going to affect my friendship with Jane? Have you even thought about that?" There is no way Paulette can tell Tina that James has been with Jane that week. Paulette starts to feel like she's living in some soap opera. Tina responds, "Look Paulette, before I leave, just remember you are letting a good friendship walk out the door."

"Tina if we are such good friends, why won't you take my advice or reconsider?"

"Paulette all my life I's had to listen to people tell me what to do, where to go, and how to dress. For the first time I's found somebody that makes me feel good, and I don't have to put on these clothes on to be accepted."

"Why didn't you tell me that's how you felt?"

"In my family, you're not allowed to show your misery. everything has to be perfect. Remember when you asked me do I ever feel alone? Well, I answered you didn't I?"

"You did."

"Do you think I was joking?"

"Well, I really didn't believe it was that serious. I saw everything that you had and not to mention how your family got along."

"Paulette everything that looks alright is not."

"Tina why don't you take your own advice and listen to what you just said."

"My mind is made up."

"Well, are you going to tell Jane?"

"I thought I would leave that up to you."

"Well think again."

"I have to go. If you tell her that's good, but if not, that's even better." Tina leaves and Paulette plops on the bed, shaking her head. Why is everything changing? How can Tina go on like she do knowing that one of her friends loves James? There's too much going on. Paulette begins to journal, writing, "Why am I taking on everybody's problems? Here I am only 17 years of age. I didn't ask to be here, but yet here I am, and I have to still make decisions and hopefully they're the right ones."

September is getting colder, and Paulette needs some winter clothes. It's only 2 p.m. and she decides to go shopping with the money she found, thinking how it really came in handy. But Paulette doesn't want to go shopping alone, so she calls Jane to see if she wants to tag along. When Paulette calls Jane, Jane answers on the second ring. Paulette is shocked to finally get a response. "Girl what happen to you?" Paulette asks.

"Paulette I am not in the best of moods. James is getting married." Paulette almost chokes before asking, "to whom?"

"Can you imagine? After all I have been through with him?"

Paulette tries to console her, "Well, you were too good for him anyways."

"That's beside the point. I really do love him. Wait until I get my hands on that snake that stole my man. I'll kill her!"

"Now hold on a minute. You're taking this way too far! You're only 17, and you haven't even begun to live."

"Paulette, I have experienced more than you can imagine and right now I don't need your lecturing."

Paulette hears her begin to cry right after she asks, "What time are you going to pick me up?" Paulette feels so confused, she doesn't know what to say. "Listen, Jane, there are so many more men out there! Some who can love you the way you deserve to be loved."

"Paulette I know but they're not him," Jane said sobbing.

Chapter 7: Why Did She Have to Leave (With No Goodbye)?

That day at the mall seems long and dreary. Jane talks and cries. Paulette keeps wondering what she should do. All Paulette can think about is whether Jane will feel betrayed by her if she tells her he's marrying Tina. By not saying anything, it will seem she is honoring her friendship with Tina instead. For once Paulette wishes somebody could give her some answers. Finally, the day ends. Paulette arrives home and notices Mark sitting in his car, waiting for her in front of the house. "Paulette we need to talk," he yells.

"About what? Mark I have called your house a couple times, and there has been no answer."

"I know. That's what we need to talk about. Listen, Babe, please don't be mad at me I had to do a little time in jail."

"What!"

"It's not what you think. I just had a couple of tickets that needed to be taken care of, but everything is a'right now."

"Do you expect me to believe that?"

"Listen I know that you're angry, but yes I do."

Paulette begins to feel like she has no friends and she really needs somebody to talk to. She tells Mark, "Mark, I just got home. I need to let my grandma know I am home OK? Be right out." Grandma is nowhere to be found, and neither is Unc. There's a note on the refrigerator telling Paulette to go to the hospital. Paulette runs out of the house as fast as possible. With tears in her eyes, she runs to tell Mark, and they rush to the hospital. Grandma's in intensive care and Unc sits with his head down.

"Unc?" says Paulette. Unc grabs for Paulette and holds on tight.

"Paulette, Why did this have to happen?" he murmurs. Unc says, "the doctor, pronounced grandma dead while I was on my way up the hospital stairs." Paulette screams uncontrollably. She feels so many emotions raging through her body all she can cry aloud is, "What in the hell is going on in my life?"

"Calm down," says Mark as he grabs and holds Paulette close. For the first time, Paulette feels that the hug is really real. As Mark comforts Paulette, she notices a red mark on his neck. "Mark?"

"Yes, Baby."

"What is that red mark on your neck?"

"What red mark?" Mark rushes into the men's restroom. When he returns from the bathroom he has a puzzled look on his face. Paulette asks him again what it is. Mark just shakes his head and replies a mosquito must have bitten him. Paulette walks away saying, "that must have been a humongous mosquito." That night Paulette stays at Marks. They have an excellent dinner, sit by the fireplace, and have several glasses of wine. Before the evening ends Paulette hears herself scream out, "Please don't hurt me!" Paulette is very hysterical.

"Paulette! Paulette!" Mark has to slap Paulette to get her to calm down.

"Mark. What is it?" That's all Paulette can say that follow morning cause Mark is looking at her with a very strange look on his face.

"What's wrong with you?"

"Do you remember what happen last night?"

"No!"

"Paulette, you thought I was going to hurt you."

"What are you talking about? You would never hurt me."

"Listen there is something you're not telling me, and I think we should come clean with each other."

"Can we talk about this some other time and by the way when will tell me how you got that mark on your neck." On the way home, Paulette couldn't help but cry.

"Paulette I think you need to go and talk to someone. I mean I am no expert, but something is definitely wrong."

"Mark who died and made you God?"

"It takes no God to know there is something wrong with this picture of your life."

"Would you please get off my back? My friends are constantly on me, and my grandmother just passed, not to mention–" Paulette catches herself before she continues. After getting out of the car, Paulette leans over in the car and tells Mark she needs to be alone for a while and will call him if she feels like company. Before entering the house, Paulette checks the mail. There's a letter from the school. When Paulette opens the letter, she sees that the letter is informing her grandmother that Paulette has not been to school. Paulette has so much on her mind that she takes the letter and throws it in the trash. Upon walking in the house, Paulette notices Unc stretched out on the couch holding an empty bottle at his fingertips. Paulette begins to shake her uncle while screaming "Wake up." Paulette sees his head move but nothing else. Paulette walks to the kitchen and opens the back door. The wind blows softly as if to say *I know what you are going through*. The leaves even fly by in a subtle way, as if they also know what she's experiencing. Paulette cries through much of the day and asks herself, *why is life so unfair*? Paulette closes the kitchen door then slowly climbs the stairs to her room. She pounces on the bed and stares at pictures of Tina, Jane, and herself. *Those seem like some happy moments,* Paulette thinks to herself. *There was a time we were happy.*

Paulette turns and looks in the mirror. It seems she has not really looked at herself in a long time. She realizes the skinny little girl with freckles is becoming a beautiful young lady. Paulette smiles. Somehow despite all her losses that create such a bottomless void within, the Paulette in the mirror is reassuring. As though somehow she knows there still can still be a life ahead of her. For the first time in a long time, Paulette finally sees who she is. Travis calls later that evening, and to Paulette, his voice is like a sweet promise that there is more for her. Travis begins to tell Paulette how sorry he is about her grandmother. Travis asks Paulette if she would like to go to church Sunday.

"Travis, not right now. It's just not the right time."

Travis said, "It's the best time. The only one who can help to ease the pain is God."

"Travis, maybe some other time."

"Okay, I will remember you said that."

The following Sunday, Paulette starts attending church, and for the first time, she begins feeling much better. After entering the house, Paulette reflects long and hard about what the minister was saying. What Paulette cannot figure out is that if God is there for her why all these bad things happen to her? Paulette drinking increases, and she quits going to school altogether. Unc tries to get Paulette to go back, but Paulette knows there's no way she will.

One day Jane stops by and Paulette says,"Hey Jane. I's not seen you for a while, how are you doing?"

"Well as to be expected, and you?"

"Well, James is getting married so that should tell you something."

"Do you know to whom yet?"

"No! However, believe you me when I do she is mine."

"What do you mean?"

"Just what I said. Nobody steps on my turf and gets away with it."

Before the conversation can continue, Tina rushes in. All Paulette can think is, *Boy* is *this a day to remember*. She says aloud, "What blew you two my way at the same time?"

"Paulette, what do you mean? We're friends," Jane responds. Paulette gives Tina a look on hearing Jane's assertion that they are all friends and hears Jane add, "I heard about your grandma passing. I'm so sorry Paulette." Tina echoes, "Me too Paulette."

"Well girls, since you are here, you might as well help me clean out my grandma's things." The whole time Paulette and Jane were together all Jane talks about is James. Paulette notices Tina is getting furious because in listening to Jane she discovers Jane and James have been together on several nights he claimed he was out with the boys. Tina turns to Paulette and tells her she has to go. Paulette can tell she is very mad about hearing all the things Jane has been saying.

As time continues to pass, Paulette sees Unc less each day. Saturdays are very rough for Paulette because her grandmother died on Saturday. Around 10:00 that Saturday morning Paulette hears a knock on the door, and upon opening it sees Tina standing alone wearing shades. Paulette knows instantly by the look on Tina's face something has happened and asks Tina about it. Tina takes her shades off reluctantly. "Tina!" Paulette yells out. "This is ridiculous you are only 17. Why do you let this guy do this and get away with hitting you?"

"Please! Don't preach to me! I don't want to hear it right now."

"Well Tina, you are a gorgeous girl. You can get any guy you want! You've got to let this scum go. I remember when we first met him and all of us were drooling over him, but for some reason, I knew he was no good. Do you ever talk to your mom?"

"Paulette, of course, I talk to my mom. Why do you ask"?

"It's just you never talk about her."

"Paulette just because I do not speak about her doesn't mean I don't talk to her." Tina then asks, "Have you talked with Jane lately Paulette?"

"No why do you ask?"

Tina begins to cry. "Paulette, you knew all along about her and James, why didn't you tell me?"

"Tina, what would you have done in my shoes? Two of my dearest friends involved with the same guy? Tina, I wanted to say something, I just didn't know how."

"Okay Paulette, I can understand that part. But why didn't you, at least, give me some clue"? While Tina continues talking, Paulette falls to her knees in screeching pain. Tina yells for Paulette's uncle. Unc runs down the stairs, finding Paulette still in a kneeling position holding her stomach and moaning. Tina and Unc help Paulette get to her feet into Unc's car. After helping Paulette into the car, Tina looks into her eyes and softly says, "Do you want me to come to the hospital with you?"

"Tina I'll be okay. Tell Jane I'll talk with her later. Please do it for me." As Paulette enters the hospital, a cold chill comes over her. This is one place Paulette thought she would never see again. Unc doesn't say a word as they approach the check-in desk. Paulette begins looking around and notices several teenagers with their sick babies. Dr. Lee calls Paulette's name before she can sit down.

"Do you want me to go in with you?" Unc asks.

"Hey, this girl will be all right. Thanks for asking." Paulette notices the doctor is looking at her with a strange look on her face. This strikes Paulette as particularly disconcerting, as Dr. Lee is a short, thin woman with curly black hair who is always smiling. Paulette feels as though she's walking through a tunnel. Once she gets to the room, Dr. Lee turns to Paulette and asks why she didn't come back for a checkup after losing the baby. Paulette looks down and shakes her head. "Dr. Lee I do not know."

"Well, let's have a look. What seems to be bothering you?" Paulette begins to tell the doctor about the pain that she has been experiencing. After listening for a while, the doctor decides to take x-rays.

Finally, the door opens. Paulette's heart began to beat quickly as the doctor walks back into the room. From the look of Dr. Lee's face, Paulette can tell something is very wrong. Paulette asks, "Is everything OK?"

"I am afraid not." She proceeds to tell Paulette what she found. Paulette burst sinto tears and runs out of the doctor's office. Paulette does not stop until she reaches the car. Unc is right behind her asking what's wrong. Paulette wants to answer but can't. Between sobbing and catching her breath, it seems impossible. Once they arrive home, Paulette barely allows the car to come to a full stop. She jumps out of the car, runs up to her room, slams the door, and throws herself on the bed. "Why Why Why?" is all Paulette can say as she cries herself to sleep." When Paulette finally awakens the phone is ringing. Paulette answers and hears Mark's voice on the other end. "Hey, lady what's the word?"

"Mark, I'm really not in the mood for your remarks."

"Touchy, Touchy. Just being a friend. Heard you were rushed to the hospital today."

"Wow, news sure does travel fast. Mark for the record, I am fine so please make sure you tell the rest of the world what I just said."

"Sure, then if you are so fine, let's grab a bite to eat later." Paulette sighed. "Mark what time"?

"Now that's my girl. Let's say I pick you up about 7:00 this evening"? Paulette looks to see the clock says 4:00 p.m.

"Sounds good. Will sees you then. And Mark, drive safely." Paulette goes downstairs and sees a note from Unc on the refrigerator that he went to the pool hall. There's a pot of stew on the stove so Paulette decides to eat a bowl. Paulette continues to eat and tries to fight back the tears. She notices a bottle of brandy sitting on the kitchen table. *Now that's strange,* Paulette thinks considering she's the only one who drinks. Or so she thought. The pain Paulette begins to feel becomes unbearable. She starts thinking about all hardships of her life, including when she discovered her parents were gone. Paulette decides to take just one

drink, telling herself it is just to ease the night with Mark. To make

sure Unc will not notice, Paulette fills the bottle with water after

taking two more drinks. While filling the bottle with water,

Paulette hears a knock at the door. She thinks, *Who could be*

coming over at this time of day. It can't be Mark. Paulette opens

the door. Jane rushes in talking fast. She needs the coat she left at

Paulettes. Paulette immediately notices Jane's bruised eye and

asks, "What happen to your eye?"

Jane murmers, "It was an accident—ran into the kitchen wall."

"How can you run into a kitchen wall?" Paulette says, "Look

Jane you really should think about your relationship."

"I really must be going. Call you later." Paulette notices James

sitting waiting for Jane in the car. *Why doesn't Tina come over*

now? Paulette thinks. Paulette shuts the door quietly and walks

back to the kitchen to take one more drink. Paulette begins to

murmur outloud, "If only my grandmother could come back to me.

I need you grandma. Why did you have to leave me?" Paulette

notices the bottle is filled with more water than brandy. What is she going to tell Unc? Paulette decides to tell Unc that she broke the bottle by accident. Paulette begins to feel pretty light headed and decides to lie down on the couch. She begins to doze and then hears somebody calling her name. It's Unc. "Paulette what happen to my brandy"?

"Please lower your voice; my head is killing me."

"I am sure it is, considering you drank a whole bottle of brandy."

"Did not. The bottle break by accident."

"Paulette you smell like a liquor barn and you going tell me it broke? Girl gets your act together. You cannot drink your problems away."

"Unc you can go buy another bottle. By the way do you have any aspirin? My head is killing me."

"If your grandmother knew this drinking was going on she would turn over in her grave."

"Well she does not know, so I am sure she will be alright, and if she did happen to find out, who would tell her, you?" Paulette tries to chuckle, but the pain in her head is too painful. The phone rings. Paulette doesn't answer. Instead, Unc walks into the living room to let Paulette know the phone is for her. "Who is it?" Paulette whispers.

"How do I know? You don't pay me to be your secretary?" Unc walks away as Paulette picks up the phone. She hears, "How is my girl doing"?

"Mark actually I just talked to you not even 2 hours ago."

"Well I miss you already, and it's been longer than that since we talked. I am on my way to pick you up for dinner."

"Listen I am really not in the best of moods."

"Well, how about I come pick you up and help you feel better?"

"How about we talk later tomorrow."

"What is wrong with you? If you don't want me calling, just say so."

"Mark, it's not you. I just don't feel like being bothered. A lot has happened in the past few days. I just need a moment. You understand?"

"OK Paulette, we can try for tomorrow." Paulette gets off the phone with Mark, yet she still feels the need to talk to Travis, so she gives him a call. Travis comes over from work about 10:00 that night. Paulette is really glad to see him and Paulette can tell Travis feels the same way. She lights up at the ice cream he brings her— her favorite, black walnut. Thank God the aspirin has kicked in. Paulette is feeling so much better. She asks him, "Travis would you like something to drink"?

"Just a glass of water."

"Travis I have not heard from you in a while. Who's the lucky girl."

"Paulette I haven't the slightest idea of what you're talking about. I've been working very hard and I do have continuation school." The way he says it she can tell the remark is targeted at her. She responds, "Listen, I know I've missed a lot of school lately, but right now I have too much on my mind."

"Paulette, you can never give up on the school no matter what happens. You have got to keep going! That's all we have on our side right now. We both gave up once."

"What do you mean?" Paulette asks, a puzzled expression on her face.

"We dropped out the first time and we are not rich. Therefore, it is going to take smarts to get us where we need to go."

"Travis, not up to lectures, just your company, is that okay"?

"Paulette, I'm just concerned about you, that's all."

"Travis, I'll be okay. Do you wanna play cards or something"?

"Paulette I have something I've been wanting to ask you? Do you think about your mother?" Paulette gets out of the chair and walks over to the window. She responds, "Travis, why are you asking me about my mother?"

"Doesn't it bother you how she died?" Paulette is inwardly furious with Travis for even mentioning her mother. She simply asks Travis to leave. But before leaving, Travis turns to Paulette and says, "Sorry Paulette. I just feel you have been through so much. You got to talk about all this stuff you been through at some point."

"At this point, I really think you should call me tomorrow." Before Travis walks out the door, he kisses Paulette on the cheek and lets her know that if she needs to talk he will always be there.

Paulette knows she's lived in denial of her feelings for much of her life. She shuts the door and begin to murmur outloud, "Who is Travis to question me at a time like this. He's just a friend. If only my grandmother were here. She could always make me feel better." Paulette decides to turn in for the night. She grabs a couple cookies before heading up to bed. Upon entering the kitchen, she sees another bottle of brandy in the kitchen cabinet. Paulette decides to help herself to another drink. She then takes a nice hot shower and drifts off to sleep.

On Sunday morning, Paulette decides to go to church again with Travis. As always, Paulette feels wonderful after service.

Sunday is spent with Paulette mulling over the thoughts of church and then drinking before turning in for the night. On Monday morning Paulette is awakened with a thump on the door. Unc is not home so she decides to go see who it is. Paulette looks through the peephole and sees two men standing in business suits. Paulette cracks the door and asks who they're looking for." One asks, "Is Ms. Thomas is there?" Paulette asks, "Who are you? Don't you know my grandmother has been deceased for a little over a month?"

"Ma'am, I do apologize for your mishap, but we are here to collect some money for back taxes."

"Back taxes? What are you talking about?"

"Well, it seems as though your grandmother allowed 3 years to go by without paying."

"What are the taxes for?"

"Well, let's see. From the information I have here, it looks like property taxes."

"Well, how much are they"?

"Looks like $5,000 to be exact."

"We don't have that kind of money."

"Listen I do understand your situation, but business is business, and if we don't receive payment by the end of this month, we are going to have to sell the house."

"Hey, this house is worth more than $5,000. My grandparents paid for this home."

"Just doing my job." Paulette takes the papers then closes the door slowly. *What are we going to do? My grandfather worked too hard to just let them take the house.* Now at age 18, Paulette thinks this is just too much for her to deal with. She lay on the couch in the living room trying to go back to sleep. Paulette tosses from side to side and just can't fall asleep. Then an idea hits her. Mark is always saying to let him know if she needs any help. Paulette calls Mark, and he answers on the third ring. "Hi, were you sleeping?" Paulette asks. Paulette begins to explain to him what's going on and asks if he can help her out.

"Help? That all depends on."

"On what?"

"If you will have dinner with me later on this evening."

"What time are we talking?"

"Do you have something else planned"

"No not really."

"Good! Then I'll see you around 7:30 tonight." All Paulette can think about is how happy she is to have a friend like Mark. There's a knock on the door interrupting Paulette's thoughts. Paulette wonders who it can be. She opens the door and sees Jane standing there with blood running down her face and arms. "Jane! What happen to you?"

"Please, I can't talk right now. Can I take a shower and lay down for a minute?"

"Sure. you know you're always welcome here." After Jane gets out of the shower, she still doesn't want to talk so Paulette fixes an excellent breakfast. While eating breakfast, Paulette and Jane finally start talking. "Jane who did this to you?"

"Please, Paulette. I really don't want to get into this right now."

"Well, can you tell me what it was about?"

"I caught James talking to another woman on the phone."

"How?"

"I wanted to make a phone call so I picked up the phone."

"You know Paulette, the funny thing is the woman's voice sounded kind of familiar." Jane begins shaking her head then adds, "I am sure it isn't anybody I know. But Paulette, I needed to know who he was talking to. So, I decided to interrupt their conversation. There was silence for a minute. I heard the phone hang up. The next thing I know James runs in the bedroom and slaps me as hard as he can. I told him I had every right to know who he was talking too. The last thing I remember is throwing a vase at him, which hit him in the face." Jane begins to cry hysterically. "Paulette, I can't believe he would do this to me." "Paulette walks over to put her hand on Jane's shoulder and asks, "You knew he was seeing somebody else right? He's getting married isn't he?"

"Yes, but to disrespect me in my own home. That's cruel."

"Jane, why don't you lay down for a while and we will continue this conversation later." Paulette feels she has too much going on in her own world to deal with more problems but also feels she has to be there for her friend. Paulette understands the meaning of friendship as she sits and thinks while Jane sleeps on the couch. Paulette calls Mark and tells him she feels she needs to help Jane and so postpones their dinner. In the end, the day is a long one. Paulette decides to go upstairs and get ready for bed, as it's getting pretty late. Approximately 9:15 pm, Mark calls to make sure Paulette is okay. Paulette feels sorrowful inside. She is beginning to feel so alone. The only friendship she feels is dependable is Travis and Mark.

Chapter 8: Silence or Choose To Tell

Jane is too wrapped up in James to pay attention to Paulette's feelings. But life for Paulette is sure not a bowl of fun. It seems like she always has to make a tough decision that could change her world for good. One, in particular, is how, or whether, she tells Jane that Tina is the other women? *There is no way* Paulette thinks *I can do such a thing. It'll ruin my relationship with Jane and Tina.* Paulette begins to feel exhausted. Before turning in for bed, she kneels down and says a prayer for all her friends and loved ones.

New York is a fun town to live in at least that is what Paulette has heard and Paulette longs to be able to enjoy the city as if she were only 15 and had no real troubles. What is there to do at such a young age? Around 2 o'clock that morning Paulette is awakened by the howling of the wind. She notices Jane has left. How could she? Before Paulette allows herself to get upset, she tries calming herself down. She goes back upstairs and gets back into bed. Sleep is difficult and all Paulette can think about is Jane. *How can you go back to this guy?* She thinks.

Alhough Paulette feels strong in her convictions, she knows her own life is just as bad. The fact of the matter is that Paulette has plenty of problems. Days go by. Wednesday around 5 that evening Unc finally decides to come home. Boy is Paulette happy to see him, but she can tell something is wrong. He doesn't look the same. Not much is said and Unc just tells Paulette they need to talk as he continues walking to his room. Paulette thinks *that's strange. Unc had not been home for several days. And yet he gave her no kiss or hug, not to mention Unc did not look happy to see Paulette.* Paulette decides it would be best to talk to him another time about the tax collectors.

Later on that evening, Paulette gets a phone call; Mark is on the other end. He asks if Paulette wants to go to a party with him. Paulette is so elated, especially because she had just sat wondering what she could do in the city of New York. Paulette is very excited to get out of the house. Leaving her worries behind, she makes up her mind that she's going to have fun. Mark picks up Paulette and they arrive at the party close to 9:30 pm. There are people and loud music everywhere. Paulette knows she is in for a real time, or so she thinks. Upon entering the house, Paulette notices Jane and James standing by the punch bowl in the kitchen. They seem to be having a heated conversation. Paulette wants to go over and speak, but Mark tugs on her hand and said, "Look she can take care of herself." Paulette agrees, reminding herself, *Who did you come here with anyways, Jane or Mark?* Paulette glances at Jane one more time before going upstairs. But before Paulette can reach the top of the stairs, there's a loud rumbling noise coming from the kitchen. Paulette sees Jane running out of the kitchen, her shirt red with blood. Before she can make it out the door, Jane passes out. Paulette rushes to her as fast as she can. Paulette calls to her several times. "Please say something. Will somebody call an ambulance?" Nobody moves. *What's wrong with these people?* Paulette thinks to herself. Paulette runs to the phone to call herself.

James grabs Paulette's arm. "Let go of my arm you are hurting me!"

James says threateningly,"Paulette, you have 2 seconds to get this female off my property!"

"How could you do such a thing? I thought you loved Jane. You will pay for what you have done."

"Paulette, I have no beef with you, so please stay out of my business."

"Listen, mister, any time you are dealing with two of my best friends, it is already my business." Jane is conscious enough to look up at Paulette and ask, "What are you talking about?" Paulette tells her, "Don't worry about what I'm saying. We're taking you to the hospital." Jane loses consciousness again and Paulette hears Mark call after her as she climbs into the ambulance. Paulette doesn't look back. She just continues climbing into the ambulance. What Jane is going through is more important than what Mark has to say. Jane is unconscious for several hours, and when she awakens it's another day. "Hey friend, are you all right?" asks Paulette.

"Do you think a little knocking around could stop me?" Jane responds.

"A little knocking around? Jane you were out for at least 10 hours!''

"Do you know what your problem is?"

"I have a feeling that you are going to tell me."

"You worry too much."

"That has been said to me on several occasions. Can you blame me? Look who I picked to be best friends with?"

"Speaking of best friends Paulette, what were you talking to James about?" Paulette interrupts her before she can finish. "Jane, you need all your strength. Don't worry about that guy. He is nothing but a loser."

"Maybe, but I still like to know, and you're going to tell me." But before Jane could say more, she dozes off into a deep sleep. Paulette feels her heart fill up with affection for Jane as she looks at her. Paulette says a prayer softly for Jane in hopes she will get better.

Snow begins to fall as Paulette walks out of the hospital. She starts to cry quietly. With everything that has and is still going on in her life, she cannot understand why she has not lost it. No matter what the situation, Paulette always talks to God, believing he will fix things after a while. As Paulette walks to the bus stop, she wonders what else could go wrong. Upon entering the house, Paulette notices a note on the refrigerator letting her know that Unc is going to be home later that evening. Paulette doesn't care. She is too tired to think or care about the money they owe. Paulette proceeds to fall on the couch and sleeps til about 10 that night. She awakens to the sound of a knock on the door. *Now who could that be at this time of night?* Paulette wonders as she slowly walks to the door to find Travis standing on the other side. "What are you doing here and why didn't you call to let me know you were coming over?"

"Hey, chill! What's wrong? I come over another time."

"I'm so sorry Travis. Please, do come in. What's wrong? Everything! Wait a minute, how did you know I would be home?"

"A little bird told me."

"Would that little bird happen to be some kin to me?"

"Maybe, but please don't be mad at him."

"I'm glad you stopped by."

"Do you mind if I stay with you tonight?"

"Not at all, I can use the company."

"What about your Uncle? Where is he?"

"Most likely he'll be home tomorrow, but don't worry, I have a feeling he would not mind one bit."

Travis and Paulette go to her room. At first, Paulette cannot get undressed. Then Travis touches her shoulder, leans over, and whispers "I want to bite you." Paulette looks into his eyes and whispers "I know." Paulette begins to get slowly undressed and jumps into bed. Travis gets in right behind her. Paulette's heart begins to beat fast. Travis puts his arms around Paulette and softly whispers that all he wants to do is lay beside her and hold her in his arms. For a moment, Paulette lay feeling a bit awkward thinking about her grandmother, thinking about what she would say, it's hard for her to imagine that all Travis wants to do is hold her. *Life is beginning to get more and more difficult each day.* Paulette cannot fight back the tears and she softly cries. Travis says gently, "Paulette, everything is going to be all right, just let it all out. God is going to take care of everything." Travis holds Paulette tighter as they both drift off to sleep. They awake around 830 a.m. Before Travis leaves, he grabs Paulette and gives her a big hug goodbye. Paulette cannot go back to sleep. She decides to get dressed and see how Jane is doing. She arrives at the hospital around 10:15 am. Before Paulette can get on the elevator, she hears Ms. Jenkins, Jane's nurse, call after her. Startled, Paulette says, "Hi Miss Jenkins how is our patient doing?"

"Paulette, Jane is not here."

"What do you mean?"

"She left about 12 a.m. last night."

"How? Why? In her condition?"

"Please calm down. The gentleman that came to get her seemed very nice. I am sure she is in good hands."

"Would you please describe him to me? How could she go back to that jerk?"

"Who?" Ms. Jenkins asks.

"Listen, Ms. Jenkins, I really must be going now." The more Paulette thinks about the situation the madder she gets. What is Jane thinking? Paulette rushes to a pay phone to call Mark. Mark always knows what's going on and always goes to James house without letting him know he's coming. Then it dawns on Paulette that today is Thursday and she has a follow-up doctor's appointment. Paulette realizes she cannot make the appointment because she has to find Jane, so she reschedules for a later day. Paulette calls Mark again only to get his voicemail. She leaves a message hoping that Mark will call back soon and decides to go home to wait for his call. Unc is home and he tells Paulette that Mark just called. Paulette quickly grabs the phone and calls back. After Paulette explains what's going on, Mark tells her she should let grown people handle their own business. Paulette feels offended by Mark's comment. She says, "Mark, I thought you were my friend."

"Baby, I am. This is just something better left alone."

"Well, that's your opinion, but Jane is my friend, and you have no idea."

"No idea about what?" Mark asks. Paulette decides not to say another word before she says something that she will regret. Paulette slams the phone down as hard as she can. She stares at the phone in hopes that Mark will call back. She looks up from the phone only to find Unc standing in front of her looking at her. "Paulette what has gotten into you? You know if your grandmother was here—"

Paulette interrupts Unc's thought as she screams "But she's not!" and she runs up to her room. Paulette lay stretched out on her bed looking up towards the ceiling. Paulette remembers what her grandmother use to say "in times of trouble say a prayer for the man upstairs cause he knows how to handle what you are going through."

It's only 12:30 p.m. and Paulette now feels she should have gone to her doctor's appointment. She feels a little tired, so she decide to take a nap. Before she can doze off, the phone rings. She hears Tina's voice say, "Hi, Paulette what's been happening?"

"Haven't you heard?"

"Heard what?"

"What happen yesterday at James house?"

"No, but I am sure you're going to tell me."

"Well, James was having this party."

"Paulette will you get to the good part already?"

"James put Jane in the hospital."

"He did what? That scum said he finished with her. If you like, you can ask him for yourself. Paulette, I know you would not lie about a thing like this. Can you imagine I was going to marry him this weekend?" Tina begins to cry.

"Marry him?" Paulette responds. "After all he has put you through?"

"Paulette, I love him. He makes me feel like I have never felt before."

"Tina, you do not even know him. Listen to what you are saying. And you're only 18."

"Paulette, why do we always seem to come back to this argument whenever we see or talk to each other?"

"Tina, I don't know but shouldn't that tell you something is wrong?"

"No Paulette it just tells me that maybe you are jealous."

"Jealous? Jealous of what?"

"Paulette, I don't know. That's for you to figure out. Got to go. Will talk to you later."

Paulette sits shaking her head. Paulette still tries to take a nap only to find sleep does not come easy. She goes to the kitchen and takes a drink of Unc's brandy. Paulette is feeling lonely. However, that day after school Travis come over with a handful of red roses.

"This is the nicest thing that anybody has ever done for me," says Paulette. Travis looks at Paulette, grabs her, and gives her a big kiss. Unc walks in. They hastily pull away from each other.

"What's going on here?"

"Oh, Unc!" Paulette says shyly, "I am no longer a little girl you know."

"Well, you may not feel like you are, but in my eyes, you will always be. Now if you both don't mind, I like to watch a little TV."

As they were walking out, they hear Unc murmuring something. Travis says, "Is your Uncle a'right? He seems to be pretty upset?"

"Oh, he be okay."

"Paulette, let's go to the movies."

"I would love to. Just let me grab my coat," she responds. She yells to Unc, "Unc, I'm getting ready to go to the movies. You do not have to wait up." The look on her uncle's face lets Paulette know he will be up when she returns.

Travis has his mother's car—a new blue Honda. Although the car is not a Corvette like Paulette is used to riding in, she feels comfortable and cozy as she sits in the passenger seat. Instead of going to the movies, they both decide to ride out to the beach. It doesn't matter that the weather is cold and windy. There are several blankets in the back seat and there's a basket that has been prepared for them to eat. Travis decides to build a fire where they both sit snuggled together, eating, talking, and kissing lightly.

The night is passing fast. There's light, but not much, and they both decide to go back to Paulette's house. Before going into the house, Travis turns and looks Paulette in the eyes. He says, "Paulette, I know we haven't known each other long. And we're both were trying to complete school, but I feel like we know and understand each other in ways that really matter." Looking deeply into Paulette's eyes, Travis softly speaks of how much he loves her. Paulette feels a hot flush come over her from the top of her head to the soles of her feet. As Paulette stands looking Travis in his eyes, she hears somebody call her name. *No, it could not be.*

That could not be Mark, Paulette thinks to herself. Travis interrupts Paulette's thoughts. "Paulette, have you heard a word I have said?"

"Yes, that you love me."

"Is that it? What's wrong? Maybe I shouldn't have said that?

"No, Mark, you should always express how you feel." *Mark! You're speaking to Travis remember?* That moment does not last very long, and no more words are exchanged. Paulette tries to explain, but Travis walks away not wanting to hear a word of what Paulette has to say.

Before Paulette goes into the house, she yells at Travis "Wouldn't blame you if you never wish to speak to me again." Travis doesn't say anything, he just continues walking back to the car. Paulette can hear Travis leaving, and she can tell he's upset.

After entering the house, Paulette gives Mark a call. Mark answers on the third ring. Paulette hangs the phone up and tries to make sense of whom she heard calling her name. Mark calls right back. "What's going on Paulette? Why hang up the phone?"

"Oh, that was an accident."

"Well? What were you wanting? Want papa to come and tell you a bedtime story?"

"Not tonight Mark, it's pretty late." Paulette cannot help but wonder about Travis. How can she hear Mark's voice when he's not around? That Friday morning Unc tells Paulette he needs to have the house to himself the day of his birthday. He and some of his church members are getting together to celebrate his birthday. Paulette tells him that she'll stay with Tina.

The weekend of Unc's birthday party, Paulette arranges to stay at Mark's. Mark agrees and said should anything change before the day of the party he'll let Paulette know. Paulette has never told Mark or Travis she was seeing them both. Mark is 25, and Travis is 19. Paulette consideres herself pretty lucky. She doesn't know what it is about Travis she likes so much. Travis is tall with reddish brown hair. He's slim, looking like he only weighs about 130 pounds, but he knows how to treat a woman, and she knows just by looking into his big brown eyes that he can charm a girl's pants off. He enjoys spending much of his time going to church. Mark, on the other hand, stays in the gym, has lots of money, is always driving fancy cars, and has a beautiful house. And he also treats her pretty good.

Early the next morning, Paulette decides to take a walk around her neighborhood, something she has never done. Paulette notices how happy some people actually look. Paulette begins to reminisce about her life and cannot help but feel lonely, empty, and confused. *Why is my life turning out to be so sour?* she thinks to herself. Paulette cannot escape these sorrowful feeings. She starts to tap into feelings she never knew were there. Paulette begins to feel a sense of anger. She feels like bringing her parents back and killing them both; her mother again. She is stunned that she would think such a thing.

Paulette continues walking and she trips over a body that's lying in the snow. Startled, Paulette jumps to her feet then returns to take a closer look. The man is old, undoubtedly homeless, with a bottle in one hand and a picture clutched tightly in the other. The picture is rather ragged looking. Paulette bends over to get a better look. Paulette cannot believe her eyes as she gasps for breath, it's a picture of Jane. *Where did he get this photo?* she thinks. Paulette beats on the man's chest in hopes he will awaken.

What is Paulette going to do? She can't leave him out to freeze to death. Rushing to a pay phone nearby, Paulette calls for an ambulance. Once it arrives, Paulette acts as if she's a family member. Curiousity gets the best of Paulette. She has to know who this old man is and how he knows Jane. Paulette decides to ride with the old man to the hospital. After waiting 45 minutes in the ER, Paulette is able to see him. Paulette walks in very slowly; she doesn't want to startle him. She notices the name tag on his wrist reads Mr. Michael Tucker. Paulette sits next to him until finally, he awakens. Mr. Tucker looks up at Paulette and asks where he is. Paulette explains what happened. Mr. Tucker expresses his gratitude. Paulette asks "Mr. Tucker?"

"Yes, child."

"Can I ask you a question? That picture you were holding. How do you know her?" Mr. Tucker looks away from Paulette. He lets out a loud sigh and does not answer. "Please, Mr. Tucker, I have got to know," Paulette pleads. Finally, Mr. Tucker looks over at Paulette, squints his eyes, and says, "She's a friend." With a puzzled look on her face, Paulette thinks this over. She doesn't recall Jane having many friends, especially anyone so old. Paulette feels she has to know more. But as she begins to ask more questions, Mr. Tucker begins to cough and gasp for breath. A couple of nurses come running in to see what was wrong. They tell Paulette she has to leave. With hesitation, Paulette walks out still puzzled. *What a mystery! I guess I will never know who the old man is.*

As she notices a clock walking out the door, Paulette cannot believe the time! It's 12:30 p.m. Paulette sees a cab sitting on the curb and decides to take it home instead of waiting for a bus. Although Paulette feels more confusion, she knows she has done a good deed for the day. *I may have saved a man's life.* She feels good about this. Snow begins to fall softly. Paulette reaches home, pays the cab fare, and walks slowly into the house, still thinking about Mr. Tucker. As Paulette enters her room, she hears the phone ringing. Then it dawns on her that she planned to spend the weekend with Mark. Paulette quickly runs to answer the phone. It's Mark, as she suspected. Paulette confirms they are still on for the weekend and gets off the phone only to call Travis. Travis is at work. Paulette asks if he can come over after work. Travis tells Paulette he will see her after work.

After such a long day, Paulette decides she need to freshen up before Travis arrives. While taking a shower, Paulette begins to think about Mr. Temple and she wonders how he's doing. Then, looking out over the backyard she sees the swing her grandfather made as it moves with the wind. She thinks of how he would push her and made her laugh so hard she almost fell off. Paulette has such a warm feeling inside. These happy thoughts begin to overtake her.

Finally, Paulette's shower ends. She takes her time getting dressed and even prepares a stiff drink to settle her thoughts to enjoy her moments with Travis. Travis arrives around 7 that evening. He asks her to go to his house saying, "There's something I want to show you." Travis lives fairly close to Paulette, but even though she has her coat on, the wind seems to blow right through. When Paulette walks into the house, she sees that his mother has fixed a nice candle light dinner. There's soft music playing in the background, gospel music. Travis takes her coat and gestures her to sit down. She reflects that Travis is rather mature for his age. Travis' father left them when Travis was no more than 3 years old. *I guess you can say that has a lot to do with his maturity,* thinks Paulette. After dinner, they watch several videos, and then Travis asks Paulette if she would like to go to a church picnic on Saturday. For a moment, Paulette sits in silence thinking how she wants to go. But then she remembers the weekend ahead is with Mark and she answers that Jane is going to be spending the weekend with her. Travis asks, "Do you think she would like to come along?"

"Well, we have plans you know. We barely get to see each other these days."

"I understand. If you change your mind let me know." Before leaving, his mother taps Paulette on the shoulder and gives her a kiss on the cheek. "Paulette, I worry so much about you."

"Why?"

"Travis talks about you quite a bit, and he always tells me to say a pray for you."

"That is sweet of you Travis." She feels a touch of warmth for them both and some regret. "Well, I really must be going. Thanks for dinner." Upon entering the house, Paulette walks to the kitchen where she finds a note posted on the refrigerator to call Mark. Mark picks up on the second ring. "What's up?" Paulette asks.

"Paulette something has come up."

"Like what?"

"I have to go out of town. My baby sister Loraine is in trouble again."

"Mark, what are you trying to tell me?"

"I will not be home this weekend."

Paulette doesn't respond. She just hangs up the phone, makes

herself another drink, then runs to her room. Paulette drinks it

down to help calm her nerves. What is she is going to do? Unc

would not dare let her stay at the house. Paulette's thoughts are

interrupted by a knock on the door. Tina is standing there in tears.

Chapter 9: The Mystery Woman Revealed

"Tina," what's wrong?"

"I cannot believe he could do this to me."

"Who? What are you talking about?"

"That piece of scum. I told him I was pregnant, and do you know what he said? Either I get an abortion, or we are through!"

"Tina, why didn't you protect yourself?"

"Protect myself? Paulette, we're supposed to be getting married. Remember?"

There is nothing Paulette can say and preaching will only make matters worse. "Paulette, can stay with me at my uncle's house this weekend?" *Wow, what perfect timing!* Paulette thinks. "Sure. No problem. Just let me pack a bag." *I am confident Unc will not mind me leaving a day earlier.* Just as Paulette is walking out the door, Unc comes home. Before getting in the car, Paulette talks with her uncle, telling him she hopes he has a great party and that she will see him on Monday.

Tina talks about James all the way to her house. "Oh, Paulette, there is something I forgot to tell you. My uncle has two girls, Michelle, who is 12, and Pamela, whose 9. I hope you are okay with being around children." Tina knocks on the door and it's Michelle who answers the door. She's tall and thin with kinky curly hair and she's stunning. Pamela is sitting at the table eating a peanut butter and jelly sandwich. She has long stringy hair and she's a little on the chubby side. Finally, Paulette is introduced to Paul. When Paulette is speechless, Tina asks, "Paulette, you all right?" Paulette doesn't respond. All she can think is Paul is the most handsome guy she's ever seen. Paul smokes a cigar, and he wears a gorgeous leather jacket. The cut of his hair reminds Paulette of a military man. Not to mention his beautiful body. Paulette can tell he spends time at the gym. "Hi, Paulette," says Paul. "Tina has told me so much about you. One thing she forgot to tell me is your age. So how old are you?" Paulette clears her throat and tells Paul she's 18. "Well, Paulette, it's a pleasure to meet you. Please make yourself at home." Paulette stares at Paul until he disappears upstairs. Tina turns to Paulette and asks, "Say, are you all right?"

"Just fine."

"From the looks of you, it looks like you're burning with fever, but it's not the kind of heat that comes with sickness." Paulette looks into the mirror, and sees that Tina is right. Paulette's whole face is flushed and she's wearing a big smile. "Tina, how old is your uncle and what do you think about going to the mall on Saturday morning?"

"Well, I don't feel up to it, but maybe that's what I need. As for my uncle, he's 35." Paulette checks her bus schedule and confirms that a bus is leaving in the morning around 10. "A bus? Paulette, don't you remember. I have a car now!"

"Girl, what was I thinking?"

In the morning, Paulette awakens to the smell of bacon. She can't believe how good the house smells. Paul has prepared an excellent healthy breakfast. Tina and Paulette leave for the mall after eating. At the mall, Paulette can't believe her eyes. Jane and

James are walking out of the jewelry store together. Paulette tries to grab Tina and take her in a different direction, saying, "Let's go," but it's too late.

"Paulette, does he think he's going to get away with this? I mean who does he think he is?" Both Paulette and Tina try walking in a different direction. And Jane is quickly approaching. "Hi, Paulette," Jane says waving her finger in front of Paulette's face. "Wow! That must have cost a fortune." Tina looks at her and then walks away. Jane says, "Never mind her. Listen, would you like to be my maid of honor?"

"I accept. When's the wedding?"

"This Sunday."

"Why so soon?"

"Paulette, we have been dating for awhile now. I think this would be a perfect time."

"Jane, as a friend, I believe there's something you should know."

"What is it ?" Jane wonders.

"Tina is pregnant."

"What are you telling me for?"

"The father is James."

"That girl will try to do anything just to keep him."

"Jane say what you want, but it's true."

"James stopped talking to her a long time ago."

"That's what he wants you to believe. Jane they were going to get married."

"Paulette, I think you are making this story up. Maybe, just maybe, you want him for yourself." Before Paulette can answer Jane walks away. Nevertheless, Paulette has the feeling that Jane believes her. Paulette shakes her head as she walks towards Tina, who is standing in front of a baby store. What can Paulette say to her? Paulette walks over and touches Tina's shoulder.

"Please, Paulette, go away."

"Tina, please."

"Paulette, there is too much going on right now. James is getting married to someone else, not to mention I'm pregnant and am having a baby alone." Tina walks away in haste and she runs towards her car. Paulette tries to catch up with her. "Tina wait!" Tina stops and turns to look at Paulette. "Paulette don't you think you've done enough? Jane is your friend."

"Me?" Paulette can't believe that she's being blamed now. "Can I at least get a ride home?" Tina agrees she owes her that much. "How can you betray our friendship for that tramp?" Paulette looks over at Tina in dismay. "Tina, I have no idea what you're saying. Jane is my friend just like you are my friend, and if you both had listened to me, you wouldn't be in this situation."

"Is that so? Well this situation would not have happened if somebody didn't want me to meet this one guy so badly."

"Oh, so now you are trying to blame me for what has happened? Listen, Tina, you can lie to yourself all you want, but the truth is that Jane had him first, and you moved right in on her turf."

"Now it's her turf. I knew you were betraying our friendship. Fine, go ahead. Be on her side." There's silence all through the car until they reach Tina's house. Paulette decides to try again to talk to Tina. "Tina, please. Think about what I am saying. I can't say I totally understand this whole situation. Look, remember when I was pregnant? I was under so much pressure until I lost my baby."

"Paulette, I have thought of everything you've been saying. All I want you to do when we get inside is pack your things. This weekend has ended."

"Tina, please, don't do this. Over this guy who is playing both of my friends? Come on. Think about what is happening. I mean really, what has he done for you besides leaving you pregnant?" Paulette catches herself and says, "Tina, I am sorry for that statement."

"Paulette that was a cheap shot, but you're right. Can you repeat that?" Paulette can't believe what she hears. "Paulette, I feel so foolish for falling for all his lies," Tina responds. Paulette says, "Tina the most important thing is to focus on the life inside of you. He or she is going to need a good mother." Paulette and Tina give each other a big hug before walking in the house. "Paulette, I am glad you are my friend." When they enter the house, they see Paul sitting on the couch reading the newspaper. He says, "Girls, I didn't hear you come in. How was your day?" Tina walks to the bedroom without responding. "Our day was all right," says Paulette, "and yours?"

"Well, let's see. Michelle and Pamela's mother came and picked them up around 4:30 this afternoon. I must say I'm having a very pleasant day. Dinner will be served shortly and my secretary will be joining us. Terry is her name." As Paulette begins to head up the stairs, she hears a knock on the door and she realizes that Terry has indeed arrived. Before going all the way up the stairs, Paulette kneels down as far as she can to get a glimpse of her. Terry has bushy red hair, and wears braces. *What on earth does he see in her?* Paulette thinks. Paulette, with a little fury in her eyes, gazes at her, feeling like she has nothing to worry about. She looks much more attractive on any day. Tina taps Paulette on her shoulder and Paulette jumps. "What are you doing?"

"Don't you know you shouldn't come behind a person like that? I could've fallen the stairs?"

"Paulette, are you spying on my Uncle?"

"Tina, don't be silly. I was just trying to get rid of this major headache." Before Paulette can gain her composure, Tina starts to talk again about James and Jane. "Paulette, I still can't believe the nerve of that guy."

"Don't you think you are overreacting just a little?"

"If I were not pregnant, I would say yes, maybe a little bit. What would you do?"

"Please, Tina for your sake, just let that guy go. Remember stress kills. Because of my mother, I lost my baby. Think about what I am saying."

"Well, I guess your right. That doesn't mean I'm not going to keep thinking about what I could do to him and that pig."

"Tina do you realize we went all the way to the mall, and I didn't get anything to wear?"

"Paulette, I'm in pain right now, and all you can think about is you. Talk about selfish."

"Tina, you know as well as I do that Jane and James were together before you ever came into the picture. As a matter of fact you weren't even in New York when Jane met James. And I remember clearly telling you not to even mess with the guy. But no, you just had to have him." Paulette hears herself telling Tina I told you so and stops abruptly. "Listen I'm sorry. I really didn't mean what I just said."

"Yes, you did. You have every right to say how you feel, even though I may not agree." Paulette tries to grab Tina to give her a hug, but Tina steps back. "Paulette, I think it best that you go home." Paulette grabs all of her things and begins heading downstairs, bumping into Paul on her way down. Paul can see Paulette has her bag and says. "Where are you going?"

"I'm going home."

"What's the rush? I thought you were staying for dinner?"

"There's been a family emergency, and I really need to be getting home." Paul grabs Paulette's hand and holds it softly. "Paulette, I hope everything is alright." Tina walks out behind Paulette. Before Paulette can get in the car, Paul yells out, "Please call just to let us know how everything turns out." Terry is standing next to him. Paulette is not sure why she feels angry that Terry is there not to mention she has to go home. "I will. I'll call you when I get home. My bus is coming, gotta go."

As Paulette approaches the house, she notices Unc sitting on the porch drinking beer. "Well, Well, Well. The lost child finally decided to come home. Do you know how worried I've been about you? I even called the police for missing people."

"Unc why would do such a thing, when you told me to leave?"

"The boys have been calling here like crazy." Paulette's eyes lit up. She's really hoping that Mark called. "Where are the messages?"

"Look on the refrigerator."

"Paulette's here," says Unc, murmuring to himself and Paulette goes into the house to look at her messages. There's no message from Mark, but Paulette notices Paul called and so did Travis several times. Paulette returns Travis' call and when he picks it up, she asks, "What are you doing home?"

"Who am I speaking with?"

"You mean you have forgotten the woman you love already?"

"Hey, girl, where on earth have you been? I've been calling you."

"I was at Tina's. So how was the Church picnic?"

"I thought you said you were going to be with Jane."

Paulette suddenly remembers she made that up and tries to cover herself with, "Tina needed me," which was the truth. Travis answers her question with, "Pretty good. I just wish you would've been there. There will be another one I am sure." Unc then stumbles into the kitchen. "Paulette, we really need to sit down and have a talk. I am the adult, and you are just a teenager who needs to really get her life together."

"Unc can't you see I am on the phone? In a minute." Paulette turns her back and continues talking with Travis. After chatting with Travis for several more minutes, Paulette ends the call and turns back to Unc, "Unc are you sure Mark didn't call?" Unc doesn't respond. He just looks at Paulette and shakes his head. "Paulette one day you are going to wish you had listen to this old man," and he stumbles on up the stairs. Paulette sits on the couch. She sees a photo album sitting on the table and with curiosity, picks it up. She sees pictures of her grandmother holding her mother when she was a infant. Paulette notices there's also a picture of herself and her grandmother. If only she had gone to the church picnic with Travis. People actually would have been shocked to see how much she had grown. Paulette begins to cry as she continues thinking about her life. Not only is her life in shambles, but her walk with God is suffering. Paulette's grandmother was a real woman of God. Paulette recalls all the times she went to church with her as a young girl. Boy did she miss those days.

Paulette walks over to the window. It seems as though every star is out shining brightly as ever. The wind is blowing, and the trees are swaying. Paulette feels that somehow they are telling her that everything is going to be alright, even though she doesn't understand when. Paulette turns her thoughts to Travis and how he is so faithful when it comes to going to church. Then Paulette wonders why he is sleeping with her if he is so much into the church? At the same time she remembers he only held her. And she also realizes she's not anyone to judge.

Paulette decides to turn in early. Her room feels so empty. Grandma tried to give the place her special touch. Paulette begins to think about Mark and the smell of his cologne. Then Paulette's mind shifts as she thinks about Travis. Paulette finally drifts off to sleep.

Early that morning, Paulette hears a loud noise. Unc is in the kitchen washing down the cabinets. "What on earth are you doing?" Paulette asks. "What does it look like I'm doing?" Unc responds. "I thought it was time that we change something around here, so I decided to start with the kitchen?"

"What do you mean? Grandma would turn over in her grave if she knew you were changing anything." Paulette yells.

"Paulette my mother would want us to get on with our lives."

"Unc you're just trying to get on with your own life. You don't care about me!" Paulette runs back upstairs. Paulette is furious. But as soon as she realizes how angry she is, she also realizes how out of sync her own reaction is. She misses her Grandmother but she realizes that Unc is making splendid sense. At the same time, she thinks, *It's too early in the day to even be thinking of any of this.* For some reason, Paulette just wants to sit and look out the window. *Tina will be having a birthday party later on that day,* she reflects. As Paulette continues looking out the window she thanks God for another day.

It's a cold day, and Paulette decides to dress warmly. She has that familiar feeling she always has when thinking of Tina and Jane fighting over James, let along her own relations between

Mark and Travis, that her life is one big soap opera. She also has no clue about where she is going or how she will get there. She falls back on her bed. Looking up at the ceiling, she wonders how Jane's doing. She hears a knock on the front door and Unc yells for her to go see who it is. It turns out to be Jane! *Boy perfect timing.* "What wind blew you my way, especially this early in the morning?" Paulette asks. "Well, I wanted to see my friend and ask if she would like to go to breakfast."

"I would be delighted. Unc is working in the kitchen so that would be great. Just let me jump in the shower and get dressed." Jane follows her up the stairs. "Paulette, there's something I would like to discuss with you." For some reason Paulette knows she came over here for more than breakfast. She also knew that one day they would have to have this talk. "Please let me say something before you go on." Paulette begins to tell Jane how sorry she is for not letting her know about Tina and James. "Really, Jane, I just didn't know how to tell you."

"Paulette, we've been friends long enough. You should know that if you ever need to tell me anything you can always say it. I'll take both the good and the bad." Paulette says, "Once again I am so very sorry."

"Trust me, if I were in your shoes, I'd probably have done the same thing," Jane replies. "Paulette, I actually want to invite you to this party tonight. Jame's brother is giving us a bridal party, even though we're already married. Would you like to come?"

Paulette thinks for a moment. "Sure. I'm not busy. That will be fun." But immediately after confirming she would attend the party the thought of Tina pops in her head. Paulette shuts out the thought, asking, "Will Mark be there?"

"I doubt it very seriously. Hasn't you heard? He's in jail."

"Jail? For what?"

"To be honest, I have no idea. James always keeps me in the dark about everything."

"That explains why he hasn't been calling me. What time should I be ready?"

"Let's say about 7:00?"

"I'll be prepared, how should I dress?"

"I would say dress beautiful and sexy. You never know, you may meet a man that will blow your mind." Paulette tells Unc that she's getting ready to go to breakfast and will be back by noon. *That's different.* Paulette realizes, *I hardly ever tell him where I'm going.* There's this great little restaurant not far away and they have a delicious breakfast. Jane and Paulette talk about everything, giong back to their early days of escape from Peter. "Paulette, what happen to us? I am only 18 and married already.

"I thought that's what you wanted."

"Well at first I did, but now I wonder if I made the wrong decision."

"Jane, you can still get out of this marriage it's never too late."

"Can I ask you one question?"

"Sure, go ahead."

"Why did you marry this guy?"

"That's the same thing that I wonder and still really don't know."

"Don't you love him?"

"Of course, I do."

"What I am hearing is something entirely different."

"Paulette is Tina really pregnant?"

"Yes, she is. I can't lie about that."

"Do you really think it's by James?"

"I really can't say."

"What do you mean? You're so close to her. Of all people, you should know. "

"Jane, did you want to take me out for breakfast for friendship or just because you want information?"

"You're right. I see what you're saying, and I'm going to put a stop to it right now. Well, are you finished? There's something I want to get at the mall for tonight."

"Can I come along? I've got to get my hair cut. It's looking awful."

"I thought you were going to get your hair cut that day that I saw you."

"Well, that's a long story, and I really don't want to get into it."

"Hey, say no more. The conversation is dropped."

"Have you figured out what you're going to do now that you're married?"

"Do like what?"

"Oh, I don't know. Are you planning on having kids?"

"No way. Not right now. I thought maybe I would take some classes in school. You know, try to get into that working world. What about you?"

"Well, I decided that I would go back to school or better yet take my GED and go from there."

"Don't you want to still become a doctor?"

"Sometimes, but there are other times I just don't know what I want to be."

"Well, don't worry. Everything will come together. It will happen before you know it."

Paulette can't help but think, *This doesn't sound like the Jane I use to talk to about what was happening. Was this marriage thing really making a difference?* Paulette goes to Your Cut and she feels so happy to be sitting in the chair knowing she's getting ready to do what she has been trying to do all weekend. She even buys a cute little outfit for the occasion.

That evening Jane and James pick Paulette up around 6:15 p.m. No words are exchanged between James and Paulette the whole time they are in the car. Jane looks back at Paulette and then James and says, "I wish somebody would say something,"

"I really don't have anything to say," James responds. *This is awkward* Paulette reflects and decides to try breaking the ice. "James tell me what I's done to make you not want to talk to me?" There's still no answer. Paulette continues to talk, saying if anybody should be mad, it should be her. Then finally James turns and looks back at her and says he has no grudge against her and everything is cool. Paulette doesn't believe a word he says, but for the sake of Jane she plays along.

Chapter 10: A Moment of Truth

There is something really strange about this area, Paulette thinks. *It actually begins to look very familiar.* A wave of sick feeling begins to wash through Paulette. Jane looks back at her. No words are exchanged, but the two understand very well what each other are feeling. Paulette asks James what his brother's name is and he tells her Pete. Instantly Paulette gets sick. James pulls over to the side of the road. Jane and Paulette stand outside the car asking what they're going to do as James walks off to relieve himself. Paulette tells Jane that it may be a coincidence and that they should still go. "You never know, it may not be him." There's a part of Paulette that hopes Jane's right and a part that knows that what Paulette knows is the truth. About 10 minutes later they pull up to the house that is the home of Pete; it is what Paulette and Jane both feared. Peter is already outside the car and Jane turns to Paulette and asks what they're going to do. James taps Jane on the shoulder from her side of the car and says, "Girls what are you waiting for?

The party is not going to come to us." But in fact, neither Paulette nor Jane want to go in. Jane finally tells James that she's not feeling well. James looks over and responds, "Don't worry, Pete has everything you need, including a bed if you want to lay down." Jane said, "That may be true, but I really would like to go home now."

"Listen, Jane, we're going to this party, and that's that." James replies. The look in his eyes let both girls know they might as well give it up and just roll with the punches. Paulette tells Jane to say a prayer and, whatever happens, they have to be strong. Pete answers the door. The look on his face shows how surprised he is to see them. "Well, little bro aren't you going to invite us in?" asks James.

"Oh sure of course come in!

"Pete, you act as if you know these girls."

"Don't be silly. Never seen them in my life," Pete responds.

"Good, I was starting to worry for a minute." As they walk in the door, both girls can hear James mumble to Pete "knowing how you do things." Paulette and Jane turn to each other wondering what that that comment meant. Does James know what Pete does for a living?

Paulette notices there are no women, at least, they aren't in sight. Jane turns and asks what or who this party is for. James says he really doesn't have a clue. "Listen, girls," James respond, "you both been acting pretty jumpy since we got here. Just chill. You're in safe hands." Of course the girls know that James has no idea what he he's talking about.

Finally Jane and Paulette are alone in the bathroom and before walking out they agree to act as normal as possible. They began to mingle with the rest of the crowd. Pete approachs them and asks how they've been doing. Neither can respond. "What girls, cat got your tongue? What's up with you two anyways? Gosh I guess some things will never change, and he begins to walk away. When he gets some distance away, he turns and asks Paulette about the baby. Paulette cannot let him get away with that cheap shot and she starts to go after him. Jane pulls her back, grabbing her arm saying, "there will be another time. We will make him pay, you can bank on that." Surprisingly, the party is entirely reasonable. Not like the parties that James and Mark take Jane and Paulette to. Pete turns the music down. He addresses the party, "May I have your attention, please? I know you all must be wondering why I'm having this party." Then Paulette notices a tall brunette walk into the room. He introduces her as his fiancée, Dedra Moons. The people in the room look very surprised. Pete explains, "I know what you all must be thinking, but there comes a time when a man must settle down." Paulette looks over at Jane and whispers that she believes he picked the wrong time, and they begin to laugh. James grabs both girls from behind. "Say, girls, why don't you have some bubbly? It will help you loosen up." Paulette can tell he has already had enough for the both of them. "Come on Paulette! This is a party," Jane blurts out. Paulette leans close to Jane and says that what she says is true, but what happens after they get tipsy? "Jane, I think we should try and stay sober if you know what I mean."

"Listen, we are big girls now. We can handle ourselves. Just relax." Jane disappears into the crowd with James, and Paulette is left to fend for herself. A guy walks up to Paulette and asks if she wants to dance. Paulette thinks *the voice sounds so familiar*. She tells him, "Maybe the next song." He then asks her if she wants a drink. Paulette thinks, *Stop acting so stiff. You are at a party. It is OK.* She says, "Sure why not?" She has two drinks and then goes on the dance floor. The way that he touches her makes her body shiver. He brings her closer and the smell of his cologne is so familiar it's as if she smelled it yesterday. "Excuse me, I did not catch your name."

"Perry, Perry Malese." Paulette seems to grasp for something to say and she comments on how fine he is. Paulette looks into Perry's eyes then asks have they ever met? "Yes, we do know each other. In my dream, I was going to marry you and take you far, far away from all this misery he responds. Paulette, you can come with me, and I will take care of you." Paulette looks up at him and begins to laugh. "Paulette I am serious." he responds. "Listen to me mister, you're fine and all, but marriage, I do not think so," she replies. No more words are exchanged and they continue to dance. When the song is over, Perry thanks Paulette for the dance and gives her a card and tells her to call him if she ever needs a friend. *At this point in my life, another friend is not what I need,* Paulette thinks, but she takes the card anyway. Then the party is finally over and as Jane and Paulette talk all the way to the house. Jane drives with her other half in the back seat passed out. "Well?"

"Well, what."

"Who was that gorgeous hunk you were dancing with?"

"Oh, Perry? He's just a guy that says he is looking to get married."

"Well, what did you say?"

"I believe I said no being that we just met, and I am not ready for that move. Just take it one day at a time. By the way, when are you and James tying the knot officially?"

"I'm glad you asked. There's going to be a double wedding."

"What?" Jane repeats what she said. "Well, with who?"

"Paulette let's discuss this another time, please?"

"Sure we can. This conversation is not over by a long shot." When Jane pulls into the driveway, Pauletee gets out. She says, "I will talk to you later Miss Lady." As soon as she walks in the house, Unc calls her name. "Yes, Unc?"

"You have not done anything, that's the problem. Look at this house, it's a mess! What would your grandmother say if she was here."

"Listen why don't you clean up since it bothers you so much?"

"Look at you. You can barely walk! Believe it or not, things are going to change around here."

"Yeah, yeah, how long have you been saying that now?"

"Don't be smart with me, young lady."

"Unc what you need is a life," and Paulette stumbles on up the stairs. But she thinks, *Who am I fooling? I know my world has to change. Too much is happening. Now that doesn't sound right either. I need to sleep this off and try thinking about it tomorrow.* Paulette finds she cannot stop thinking about Perry. *Who is this guy? It seems as though I've seen him before, but where?* Then she finally drifts off to sleep.

Sunday morning comes awfully quick and for some reason, it's freezing. *Why doesn't Unc have the heat on?* She wraps herself in her robe and puts her house shoes on. Unc is nowhere to be found. There's no note. He's just gone. Paulette begins to panic. It looks like it has been raining, and Unc hates being out in the rain. She thinks, *Well, he's a big boy. There's no need for me to worry. I'm sure he's fine.* She fixes a lovely breakfast of pancakes, bacon, and eggs. Then she turns the heater on and watches television until late that afternoon. *I hope Unc is not mad at me for how I talked to him last night.* Paulette thinks to herself. The phone rings, and the sound interrupts her thoughts. Tina is on the other end. "Well, Missy how was the party?" Paulette is stunned. *How would she even know about it?* She says, "Who told you?"

"Word gets around. Tell me how the party was?"

"Tina, I am not in the mood to discuss this, and I am sure you know why?"

"Why, whatever do you mean?"

"Tina, call me back when you are through playing this game." Paulette hangs the phone up, and Tina calls right back. She apologizes, explaining her feelings of jealousy because she was not there to enjoy the fun. "I don't know how much fun it was being confronted with my past, but I did meet a nice guy."

"Really? What is his name?"

"Perry. Very nice guy. Hey, I thought you were still mad at me?"

"Paulette, we cannot stay mad at each other. We're real friends."

"Sometimes I wonder."

"What do you mean by that?"

"Seems like since you've gotten pregnant, you've changed."

"I know my mood swings are awful and not talking to James does not help one bit. But guess what Paulette? I've decided to a take my GED. I figured with the baby coming and all, I'm going to have to be able to provide for the both of us.

"How's your mother taking the news?"

"I haven't told her."

"Why? Won't this be her first grandchild?

"Like she really cares. Anyway, who needs her."

"Tina everybody needs a mother and father no matter if there has been a problem in the past."

"Sounds like you miss your parents."

"Very much so, especially my grandmother."

At that moment Unc walks in. "Tina, call me back in about 30 minutes. I need to talk to my uncle." She turns to him and asks, "Where have you been? Don't you know I was worried sick? and why didn't you—

"Paulette calm down. I went to church with Travis. There was a men's breakfast that was at 7:30 this morning."

"Unc are you mad at me?"

"Whatever gave you that idea?"

"I'm sorry about the way I was talking to you last night."

"Listen, we are family. And yes, I get mad when I see your life being wasted."

"Unc I know you're only trying to help me, but trust me, everything is going to be alright."

"Paulette for your sake I sure hope so."

"Did Travis ask about me?"

Unc hesitated and then responded, "No. I tell you, you guys are such a trip."

Tina calls back and asks if Paulette wants to go shopping for baby clothes. Paulette says she does, and Tina says she'll pick her up around 4:30. Even though they donn't having licenses, Tina and Jane are always driving.

New York is a cold place, but something is always happening. Even in the winter, there are pimps and prostitutes walking the streets. And the funniest things happen. On the way to the mall, Paulette notices a girl standing on the corner. A guy is trying to get her to come over to the car. Finally, she goes over to him. The guy gets out the car and puts handcuffs on her. Paulette has never seen anything like that. Paulette encourages Tina to take a closer look. Paulette is shocked when she sees that it's Jane. Jane is yelling and screaming at this guy. Paulette asks Tina to stop the car, and Tina stops the car. Paulette jumps out of the car, runs over to Jane, and asks her what's going on. "Paulette," says Jane, "this guy is arresting me for solicitation."

"What! Soliciting what? Your body?" The police look over at Paulette while grabbing Jane around her arm. "Sorry to break up the party, but we must be going," and he proceeds to put Jane in the car. "If you want to talk, she may call you with her only phone call." Then he chuckles and puts Jane in the car. *If he wasn't the law, I'd tell him off,* Paulette thinks to herself as she runs to get back in the car. Before Paulette can get into the vehicle, Tina asks what's going on. Paulette fills her in on everything. "That's awful!" Paulette is glad to see the concerned look in Tina's eyes; she knows that a part of Tina feels for Jane. Paulette looks out towards the sky and murmurs, "James is a dog. Why didn't I see him for what he is?"

"What's going to happen to Jane," Tina asks.

"I don't know, but I should be home just in case she calls."

"I hope everything is all right. Well, Paulette, whatever happens, I'm sure she'll keep in touch. I sure hope so. Well so much for baby shopping. Maybe we can go tomorrow." Tina rushes off after dropping Paulette off. Paulette can tell she wants to break the news to James before anybody else gets a chance to. *What's going to happen to Jane?* is all Paulette can think. Paulette dares not tell her uncle what happened. That news would only put a notch in his belt to help prove he's been right all along.

She gets home to find out there have been no phone calls all day. *What's going on?* Paulette wonders. She doesn't feel like being alone, so she calls Perry. He's not home, so she leaves a message for him to call her back. All that evening Paulette waits for the phone to ring, but there's no call all evening. Then finally around 9:00 o'clock that night, the phone rings. It's Jane calling collect. "James is going to kill me." Jane laments. "James! How can you think about him? He's the reason you are in this mess in the first place!"

"That's not true," Jane replies. "Listen Paulette, they're telling me I have to get off the phone. Can you come and see me tomorrow early?"

"How early?"

"About 8:00?"

"Sure, I'll be there. In the meantime, you need to make up your mind and try to figure what you're going to do."

"Paulette, please say a prayer for me."

Paulette hangs up the phone and she shakes her head as she lets out a long sigh. *What is my world coming to*? Paulette thinks. Paulette will be turning 19 in a couple of days and she feels life has not been fair. That night Paulette cries herself to sleep. The next morning, Unc fixes Paulette a wonderful breakfast. "Unc why are you still here? I thought you were going to start a new job today."

"Paulette, now that momma is gone, I just didn't feel up to going to work, and I am worried about you child."

"What do you mean?" Paulette asks. Paulette helps herself to a second helping of grits and eggs. "Paulette, you are soon to be 19, and the bottom line is you have to take more responsibility for your life. All these boys and parties is just not what is happening. Look, I knows life has been tough, but Paulette, you have got to finish school or get a GED. Your grandfather believed in you child, and if your grandmother knew what has become of your life" Unc's voice trails off. He cannot complete his thought and he just shakes his head and walks away. Paulette stops eating and cries out to at her uncle. Then she asks him what's happened since he went to church. "You have been acting very strange."

"Let's just say my eyes are open, and I should be handling your wellbeing better that is what God put me here for," he responds. Paulette begins to sniffle as she thinks of her grandmother and she starts to remember how she always would tell her to trust God. Paulette begins to nod her head in confidence and agreement that she will become that person of greatness her grandfather and grandmother said she would be with the help of God.

Sunday Paulette decides to go to church with Travis hoping to gain strength and direction from God to help fuel her purpose. Pastor Jesse is preaching from John 3:16 (discussing how God so loved the world that he gave his life). Afterward, Paulette decides to go up for the altar call. Pastor Jesse begins to minister to her. On that Sunday, the day of her 19th birthday, Paulette gives her life to God.